Oboemotions
What Every Oboe Player Needs to Know About the Body

G-7367

Oboemotions

What Every Oboe Player Needs to Know about the Body

Stephen Caplan, DMA

GIA Publications, Inc.

Chicago

G-7367

Oboemotions:

What Every Oboe Player Needs to Know about the Body

Stephen Caplan

Copyright © 2009
GIA Publications, Inc.
7404 S Mason Ave
Chicago IL 60638
www.giamusic.com

Design: Robert Sacha

ISBN: 978-1-57999-727-4

Table of Contents

Foreword

Oboemotions: What Every Oboe Player Needs to Know about the Body is part method book, picture book, anatomy book, and practice handbook. Its purpose is to place the musical and technical study of the oboe within the context of a precise understanding of the human body.

The interaction of a person with a musical instrument can be a magical event. Cognitive and physical skills combine in sophisticated ways and craft beautiful musical performances. When either cognitive or physical skills are deficient, this potentially magical event becomes a disaster. Or, even worse, boring.

Unfortunately, much music training has been based on inaccurate information about how the body works or has completely ignored the body's role in making music. *Oboemotions* aims to correct this oversight. It is intended mainly for oboe players, providing very specific details related to playing techniques used for all the instruments of the oboe family: cor anglais, oboe d'amore, musette, bass oboe, and heckelphone as well as the various historical and ethnic relations.

I hope other musicians will find this book useful, particularly other wind players. I have drawn on my experiences of teaching a wide range of musicians—not just oboe players—but also flutists, bassoonists, pianists, violinists, singers, conductors, and many others. It has been supremely gratifying to witness the powerful changes these students made as they grew to better understand how the body creates music. This understanding brought about significant improvements in performance, increased personal confidence, and in many cases, relief from pain or injury. I hope that this book will help many others as they better understand how the body actually works when making music.

Oboemotions is meant to appeal to students of all ages as well as professional players and teachers. You may choose to read it from cover to cover all in one sitting. But it can also be read in sections, perhaps reading just a few pages at a time before practice sessions, then immediately trying to incorporate any new information into your practice. The spiral binding format makes it easy to place on a music stand so that you can play the musical exercises or leave it open to a figure that deserves further study.

I approach this material from a variety of perspectives—telling stories, suggesting specific musical applications, providing detailed facts, and offering visual imagery. My aim is to bring greater clarity to this information via these different perspectives and thereby engender a deeper understanding of the importance that the mind/body connection makes in musical performance.

Acknowledgments

The various case studies presented throughout *Oboemotions* are fictional. They feature characters based on composites of actual students with whom I have worked.

I am thankful for all my oboe colleagues. Some of you have been my teachers, some, my students, others have performed in chamber music or orchestral settings with me, and many of you have inspired me through your performances and recordings. I have learned and continue to learn from you all. The oboe attracts a diverse and always interesting group of compatriots, and I am glad to be a part of this family.

I am particularly grateful to Barbara Conable for her guidance and her support of this project. I am also blessed with the unending support of my family. My parents endured the early quacks and squeaks that are inevitably part of an oboist's training, and invested much time and money in helping to get me beyond that stage. My wife continues to inspire me, and served as a perceptive editor of this text. My three daughters remind me every day that the future holds great promise.

Finally, I am grateful to Gregg Sewell for his sage editorial advice and to Robert Sacha whose book design and layout brings clarity and creativity to the text, as well as to Benjamin Conable and Tim Phelps for their excellent illustrations which continue to enlighten my understanding of the body.

Chapter 1

Introducing a Somatic Approach to Oboe Playing

Oboemotions

oboemotions /o-bo-'mo-shens/ *noun*

    1: the motions and emotions of oboe playing

    2: a somatic approach to oboe playing

    Examples used in a sentence:

- Her effortless performance of the Strauss *Concerto* was due to hard work and excellent oboemotions.
- Because of his faulty oboemotions, he probably will never play *Scala di Seta* well, even if he has a hundred years to practice.

Oboemotions. You won't find the definition in a dictionary. I invented it. Why burden our vocabulary with this new word? Because it expresses a concept no other word describes. I have been studying oboe playing for more than thirty-five years and teaching it for more than twenty years. Over that time I've heard a lot of talk about the oboe from teachers, colleagues, and students—all kinds of oboe talk: talk about music, auditions, and of course, making reeds. But rarely do I hear about movement: how to move better in order to make better music, perform better auditions, and scrape better reeds.

Yet through work done with myself as well as with students, I've made an important discovery: The quality of movements a performer makes affects every aspect of performance in profound ways.

Think about it—without movement, there would be no music. On the surface, oboe players don't appear to move as much as other performers. We don't use our arms to make the overt movements of string players and pianists. Our feet don't move in the ways that organists' and timpanists' feet have to move. But the truth is we are constantly making fantastically intricate and coordinated movements to produce beautiful sounds. We move our fingers and our arms, the muscles of our face, the tongue. We move at the hip and ankle joints. The movement of

> The quality of movements a performer makes affects every aspect of performance in profound ways.

breath involves moving ribs and muscles of the abdominal walls and pelvic floor coordinated with a gathering and lengthening spine. Oboe players actually move a lot.

Movement hasn't been ignored altogether by oboe pedagogues. But unfortunately, much of what is taught about movement is misleading or inaccurate. Misconceptions about how the body actually works in movement are rampant in the music world. Making matters worse are the many phrases commonly used when teaching wind players, such as "breathe from the belly," or "column of air," or "play with an open throat." These phrases are not based in reality, and in many cases cause students to do counterproductive and sometimes harmful things to their bodies. *Oboemotions* includes discussions of many of the common myths about oboe playing. I give reasons why the myths may work for some people and why I think they are dangerous as generalizations. I also give suggestions for replacing these myths.

Myth Buster

Oboe players shouldn't move a lot.

Why this myth has helped some people:

Many beginning oboe students move inefficiently, using extra movements that are not necessary to produce music on the instrument. Sometimes these motions actually inhibit good music making. When told by teachers that oboe players aren't supposed to move much, students start to pare down excess motion and find the essential movements necessary for good performance.

How this myth is harmful:

Students begin to think that good oboe playing is a static event, which it definitely is not. Embouchures and faces become immobile, arms are held rigidly, and breath is constrained. Often this lack of mobility results in pain or injury.

Myth Replacement

Oboe players, like all musicians, are movers! Movement is necessary in order to produce sound; complex movements contribute to the complex sounds that oboe players make—sounds inspired by Bach, Britten, and Berio. There are many external and internal movements that create a good performance. These must be identified and made a part of the student's conscious awareness so that playing improves.

Creating the word *oboemotions* aligns oboe playing with movement. Just as Tchaikovsky and Beethoven inspire good oboe playing, oboe players recognize that quality motion also inspires good oboe playing.

Instead of inventing a new word, I could have written the phrase "oboe motions" simply as two separate words. Why have I linked them? Because hidden in this new word, *oboemotions*, is the all-important word *emotion*. The word *oboemotions* forever links players' emotions to their physical motions. Oboists must work to find precisely the right motions needed to play the instrument while never losing sight of the emotions that guide these motions.

Emotion is sometimes described as "moving the feelings." For good oboe playing one must access both kinds of movements—emotional and physical. They really are inseparable.

We've all experienced a performance in which the performer seems to be doing all the right things but doesn't communicate anything. Other performers communicate very expressive music in spite of their gestures. But we don't fully enjoy this sort of performance either, because the player's uncoordinated gestures make us feel uncomfortable. A great oboe player must be conscious of how physical movements relate to the movement of feelings. The motions required to bring out the ardor of the expressive oboe solo in Strauss's *Don Juan* are very different from those needed to create the joyful staccato of Rossini's *Scala di Seta*.

> A great oboe player must be conscious of how physical movements relate to the movement of feelings.

Somatics

somatics /so-'ma-tiks/ *noun*

1: body awareness

2: the study of the body in movement; typically refers to the musculoskeletal frame as distinct from the nervous or visceral systems of the body

3: the subjective experience of movement

Oboemotions is based on the concept that the feelings related to oboe playing are inseparable from the bodily movements used to produce sounds. When working with students who move awkwardly while playing music, I will sometimes ask them to feel the emotion behind the music more deeply. I have them pinpoint exactly what the emotion of the phrase is, and then to imagine how the phrase sounds when played with this emotion. With this new insight, these students play the music. Often their movement immediately improves, becoming more in sync with the music making.

Finding good oboemotions requires the following approach to practicing:

1. Find the emotion (mind)
2. Find the motions that best bring out the emotion (body)
3. Repeat these motions with emotion (mind/body)

More detail on this approach is given in Chapter 18: Practicing Oboemotions.

Oboemotions addresses the quality of movements used in all aspects of oboe playing. It analyzes in great detail what it takes to become an "embodied" oboe player. This information is not meant to replace the traditional technical basis required to be a great oboist. Barret, Gillet, Rothwell, and others have given us important technique exercises which, when mastered, make us better players. *Oboemotions* provides a firm, somatic foundation for any technique.

How often do we feel limited by our own abilities—or the lack of them? We can practice until we're blue in the face (for oboe players this cliché is quite literal), yet it seems we'll never be able to tongue fast enough, or play *Tombeau de Couperin* cleanly, or get through the solo in Tchaikovsky's *Symphony No. 4* without sounding strained. In many cases, the reason is that, regardless of how much we practice, we do it with the *same movements every time*. *Our* movements. These movements are not able to efficiently accomplish our goals because they spring from faulty habits of standing, sitting, holding the instrument, blowing into it, and the like.

Athletic training is based on finding better movements to accomplish goals. The golfer's swing, the tennis player's serve, and so forth—all are improved with a better understanding of movement. When musicians realize that they are movers, too, they begin to understand and train movement more like athletes. Oboists who understand that they are movers work differently. When they have a problem, such as playing the opening of the Mozart concerto accurately but with style, they search for better motions that allow them to reach this musical goal rather than just practicing more.

When we understand which movements are inappropriate and we change those movements, then we find the path to technical progress. This is why throughout *Oboemotions* I explain how the body works in movement followed by annotated musical examples designed to help increase awareness of movement during daily practice.

There are a wide variety of disciplines that explore the mind/body connection. Two which many musicians find helpful are Alexander Technique and Feldenkrais Method. Musicians are also drawn to yoga and tai chi, ancient disciplines based on philosophies that never acknowledged a distinction between mind and body. I have had varying degrees of experience with each of these and they have had an influence on my work; but the development of oboemotions is most deeply rooted in my study of Body Mapping.

The Body Map

body map

: one's self-representation in one's own brain. If the body map is accurate, movement is good. If the body map is inaccurate or inadequate, movement is inefficient and injury-producing.[1]

Body Mapping

: the conscious correction and refining of one's body map to produce efficient, graceful, and coordinated movement[2]

Body Mapping is the process of discovering what one's personal body map is, then consciously working to correct any mistakes found in this map in order to produce efficient, graceful, and coordinated movement. It is based on the discovery that each of us has a representation in the brain of how our body is put together. This representation is called the *body map*. This conception of how our body organizes itself actually governs the quality of our movements. If we happen to have a body map that is accurate, we move well. But when the body map is slightly off, then movement suffers. If the body map is completely off-base, then movement is awkward and injury producing.

The good news is that we are not stuck with our body maps. An inaccurate body map can be changed. Body Mapping uses a variety of methods to help you access your personal body map and then learn to correct any problems that may exist so that movement is improved.

To move well, it is important to have a body map that is accurate as well as adequate. Your body map must adequately inform you about all the things you need in order to accomplish your goals.

I just took a trip to Zion National Park. I found my favorite map program on the internet and got directions. The map I downloaded showed various highway connections needed to reach my destination. But then I decided to make a side trip to St. George, Utah. Although I passed right by St. George to get to Zion, my map did not give me detailed street directions for this city, so I downloaded a second map to find out how to get around.

Our body maps can work the same way. A violinist can get by perfectly well without mapping the tongue, but an oboist must have an accurate understanding of the tongue in order to play the instrument. In fact, there are many body maps of which oboists need to be aware. I've invented an acronym for some of the most crucial areas for which oboe players need accurate maps, and I devote a chapter to each of these areas. It is a *F. E. A. T.* to play the oboe—one must accurately map **F**ingers, **E**mbouchure, **A**ir, and **T**ongue.

> The conception of how our body organizes itself actually governs the quality of our movements. If we happen to have a body map that is accurate, we move well. But when the body map is slightly off, then movement suffers.

But each of these elements must be understood in the context of a whole body.

Body Mapping—Why Not?

Barbara Conable developed Body Mapping with cellist Bill Conable. She is a highly respected Alexander Technique teacher who has helped hundreds of musicians improve their performance. She has worked with many musicians who have experienced injury from playing music and has saved many musical careers. She established Andover Educators, a network of musicians trained to teach Body Mapping, as well as the course "What Every Musician Needs to Know about the Body." Body Mapping is the result of a lifetime of research, observation and hands-on work with a wide variety of musicians. Although much can be learned from just reading information about Body Mapping, actually embodying the information and making it a part of one's performance is best done with an Andover Educator's guidance. A list of currently certified Andover Educators can be found at www.bodymap.org

Body Mapping is logical and easy to understand. But some people feel it isn't necessary to learn anatomical information in relation to music making. They feel too much information clouds one's musical vision. This is one reason why I consistently stress the link between the emotion of the music and the physical motion needed to create the music. In performance you're not thinking about anatomy; you're focused on sounds coming out of the instrument, and on using those sounds to tell a story. Because of the way you've practiced for the performance, however, it will be second nature to produce good sounds by using appropriate movements, and you will only need to shift your awareness to physical matters if you hear that you're getting into trouble.

Some musicians want to avoid understanding anatomy and movement, making the analogy that you don't need to be a car mechanic to drive a car. True, if you just want to drive the car around the block. But a race car driver has a mechanic as a full-time staff member.

Most musicians want to be the best they can possibly be. Athletes and dancers have long recognized the need to understand the mechanics of the body in movement in order to perform at their best and stay healthy. Musicians use their muscles in just as sophisticated a fashion, and they expect to have careers that last quite a bit longer than most athletes and dancers. So why shouldn't musicians also have the advantage of this information—especially if it helps avoid injuries which could threaten one's career altogether?

Some argue that musicians can study Body Mapping diligently, but are so bound by postural habits that no matter how much they intellectually understand the information they are not able to effect change without the help of another person (Alexander teacher, massage therapist, Feldenkrais teacher, etc.). The only answer I can give to this is that I have personally witnessed dozens of people who have been able to make powerful changes through understanding Body Mapping alone.

I do encourage people to seek out other somatic disciplines when studying Body Mapping. The Body Mapping work will sometimes go much faster this way. In certain cases there really is a limit to the change some persons can make on their own, so supplementing Body Mapping with other work may be necessary. The beauty of Body Mapping is that it provides a foundation for better understanding and embodiment of any of these ancillary disciplines (Pilates, yoga, tai chi, Alexander Technique, etc.) so that the Body Mapping student is able to assimilate these principles more effectively.

F. M. Alexander (for whom the Alexander Technique is named) in his book, *The Use of the Self*, states, "It is the lack of valid criterion as to what constitutes right use in the sense of 'right for the purpose' that renders people unable to carry out their resolutions and to make certain changes for the better in themselves and in their conduct and attitude toward others."[3] Through the study of Body Mapping, one can gain the "valid criterion" Alexander speaks of. He ends this book with a question: "If a technique which can be proved to do this for an individual were to be made the basis of an educational plan, so that the growing generation would acquire a more valid criterion for self-judgment than is now possible with the prevailing condition of sensory misdirection of use, might not this lead in time to the substitution of reasoning reactions for those instinctive reactions...?" I believe that Barbara Conable's course "What Every Musician Needs to Know about the Body" is the realization of Alexander's educational plan. She emphatically states that the purpose of Body Mapping is to put music education on a firm somatic foundation.

Many musicians have suffered injuries from music making or play in pain. Often people in pain will find relief through a chiropractor, or Rolfing, or the wealth of other massage therapies available. Some people's habits have gotten them into such serious trouble that they require surgery to correct spinal ruptures, carpal tunnel syndrome, bone spurs, etc. The relief from surgery or therapy is often temporary, for if these people continue to misunderstand their bodies and move according to the old postural responses that caused them to visit the therapist to begin with, it won't be long before they get into trouble again. Body Mapping gives people easy-to-understand information that can bring about new ways of moving and prevent future injuries.

Some people will not need the information in *Oboemotions* in order to play better. They already have body maps which are completely adequate for good oboe playing. We often refer to these performers as "naturals." Although they may not need this information in order to improve their own performance, they will find Body Mapping quite helpful when teaching. It's often difficult for someone who has come by their ability "naturally" to understand how to help others in a meaningful way. *Oboemotions* gives teachers a vocabulary for providing guidance to a wide variety of students.

Many who read *Oboemotions* will find some information very helpful, but other information will seem so obvious that the reader will wonder why it's included at all. The fact is that something which is perfectly obvious to one performer will often be a revelation for another.

When doing any kind of work like this, one must come to the best understanding possible about one's own body and habits. There are people with anomalies that must be dealt with in unique ways. I've worked with musicians who have extra disks in their spines, one leg longer than the other, scoliosis, spinal disks congenitally fused together, double-jointedness—the list goes on. I've also worked with many students who insist they have unique problems that force them to play the oboe in a nonstandard way when in fact they are just being stubborn. The truth is that most bodies move in pretty much the same way—the manner presented in this book. Even some of the anomalies I've just listed won't prevent people from sitting and standing in the balanced way prescribed by *Oboemotions*. The movements of breathing should work in the same coordinated fashion for all of us.

Sometimes the information one gets from Body Mapping can effect an immediate and permanent change in performance. Great! Other information, however, requires our patience and perseverance in order to truly embody it—days, weeks, even years. A lifetime of personal habits have molded muscles and connective tissue into bonds that simply will not change overnight. Body Mapping provides one with an appropriate goal, but it will take persistence to bring about dramatic change. This should not be demoralizing for musicians. We are used to things working this way. We didn't pick up the oboe and expect to be playing Pasculli variations a week later. We truly understand that "slow and steady wins the race," and most of us have already experienced dramatic musical and technical achievements since those first few quacking noises we made.

My personal journey with Body Mapping has completely transformed every aspect of my playing and teaching. There have been times when I've gotten very excited because I'm finally feeling some aspect of my playing in a completely different way kinesthetically. But then this new awareness leads me to discover a deeper layer of physical problems that I must chip away at. Instead of getting depressed, I move on. I celebrate one victory, and use it to empower myself to take the next step of the journey. A journey I'm still enjoying.

Know Pain? Retrain

Many people study Body Mapping because they were playing in pain. Through Body Mapping they have learned to work *with* their bodies instead of *against* them, and have begun experiencing what a pleasure it is to make music pain-free. The cliché "no pain, no gain" is usually well-intended advice meant to encourage and inspire. Perhaps it's linked to the long-standing democratic ideal that anyone who works hard at something—puts "blood, sweat, and tears" into it—can achieve the American dream. While this

If you work with your body, not against it, you can play without pain.

cliché may resonate in certain situations, musicians should steer clear of it. "No pain, no gain" may be meaningful for weightlifters, but pumped-up muscles are not needed to play a musical instrument; tremendous muscular coordination and flexibility are. Flexibility and coordination are severely compromised when pain is present.

Some common places double reed players feel pain are lips, fingers, wrists, jaw, throat, neck, back, and abdomen. Many double reed players learn to live with these pains. Some think this is the price you must pay for being a musician. Some feel if you "work through" the pain, then you become a better player (better endurance, faster fingers, etc.). Other oboists just give up playing altogether. And some are forced to give it up, temporarily or permanently, when an injury occurs. Common injuries found among oboe players are tendonitis, tennis elbow (lateral epicondylitis), carpal tunnel syndrome, TMJ dysfunctions, and spinal disk problems.

Feeling pain should be understood for what it is—a signal from your body that something is wrong. In some cases, pain is the result of a medical problem that must be treated by a medical professional. Musicians who are in pain should always seek the opinion of a qualified medical specialist. However, in many cases pain results from habitual misuse of the body. Once you discover the cause of the pain, you can replace your old pain-provoking habit with a new habit based on freedom and ease of movement. If you work *with* your body, not *against* it, you can play without pain. Know pain?—Retrain. The phrase "no pain, no gain" must lose meaning for musicians. If you know pain, then you should retrain. And *Oboemotions* is intended to give you the means to retrain.

Playing the oboe should never be a pain in the neck (even though some oboe players are)!

Why did I study Body Mapping? I did not come to it because I had suffered an injury from playing the oboe, nor did I experience any pain when performing. I simply wanted playing to be easier. As a professional musician I was performing at a very high level, yet I felt my playing habits made performing much more difficult than it had to be. Like so many others, I had been told the oboe was "the most difficult instrument to play," so I was making it so. After reading Barbara Conable's book, *What Every Musician Needs to Know about the Body*, I knew Body Mapping was the path that could bring greater ease and freedom to my playing. I received a sabbatical from my teaching job and began studying privately with Barbara Conable. I am now a certified Andover Educator. I teach a college-level course and give master classes and private lessons based on Body Mapping.

The oboe is not the most difficult instrument to play, but some of us make it that way.

Body Mapping has improved my oboe playing in just about every way. I have more control and consistency, I can double tongue faster, I can play phrases much longer without feeling tired. I'm even making better reeds! Most importantly, I feel better when I play because I have learned how to make oboe playing easier by increasing my awareness and understanding of movement. This has given me more physical and mental freedom to play expressively.

I've written *Oboemotions* because I understand first-hand how a somatic approach can powerfully transform performance skills.

Chapter 2

Inclusive Awareness

Kinesthesia

kinesthesia /kin-uhs-'thee-zhuh/ *noun*

1: movement perception

2: an internal sense that also tells us about our size and position

3: our sixth sense

Most people are taught only five senses. It is a shame, because when something is not named it tends to be overlooked. Kinesthesia is a real thing that exists in every one of us. By naming it a sixth sense, it gains the equal importance it deserves alongside the other five senses. People who acknowledge the importance of the movement sense have taken the first step toward conscious control over a lifetime of postural habits that may be limiting or leading them toward pain and injury.

Music conservatories have been actively training three of our senses for years—seeing, touching, and hearing. Now many prominent music schools are understanding the need to train kinesthesia as well, and have begun introducing courses to address this need.

Musicians have many things on their minds while performing. They must be aware of rhythm, intonation, fingerings, dynamics, articulations, phrase gestures, following the conductor, paying the bills, and where they're going after the performance, just to name a few! In this book, I advocate for many other things which deserve equal attention but are often ignored. Kinesthetic things.

Do you presently have an awareness of your back as you play? of your atlanto-occipital joint? your feet? Noticing these things is every bit as important as noticing intonation if you want to give a fluid, embodied performance. Barbara Conable says, "When musicians conceive the sound they want to make they must also, simultaneously, conceive the movement that makes it."[4] But how can you effectively notice more things when your mind already feels overcrowded?

> "When musicians conceive the sound they want to make they must also, simultaneously, conceive the movement that makes it."
> —Barbara Conable

Inclusive awareness is the answer. Inclusive awareness, or inclusive attention, is sometimes described as mindfulness or a fluid gestalt. It is not concentrating; it is not scanning. Concentrating involves bringing all your awareness to one object at the expense of the rest of your experience. Scanning is merely sequential concentrating—bringing all your attention to one object, then another, etc.

An inclusive attention permits everything in the moment to be a part of your experience. This includes external factors such as the music you are working on and the acoustic of the space you are playing in, as well as internal factors, such as emotions, kinesthesia, or hunger.

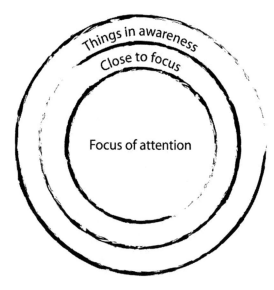

Figure 2.1. *Concentric circles*

Inclusive awareness can be represented as concentric circles. The innermost circle represents the focus of your attention in the moment. This is enclosed in a larger circle representing those things which are close to focus. The outer circle contains things in awareness, but not necessarily important in the moment. Anything can flow into the focus of the innermost circle as it is needed.

As a musician, your awareness includes the music—its rhythms and phrasings. But you are also attentive to yourself, all your psychological and emotional baggage, as well as kinesthetic and physical sensations. The physical environment—space, temperature, audience—also impacts you. At times certain elements demand greater awareness than others, shifting between the ever-widening circles. The fluidity of the circles is what keeps inclusive attention from being exhausting.

The great conductors—some of whom still exist—have the whole orchestra in their awareness all the time. Even though at one moment they may need to give the cellos an extra-vivid cue or the next moment encourage an English horn player to project more, all is done with a sense of the collective and how each element coordinates with the whole.

There are some things in our consciousness which we'd like to ignore—like a judge at a competition, or a music critic (or the conductor!). Some people recommend blocking these things out of awareness. However, it is counterproductive to try to block something completely out of awareness. It takes more work for your mind to constantly block something out than it does to just acknowledge something—accepting it when possible. You can learn to allow the judge to be there, occupying an outer circle, but not becoming the focus of your attention.

Our practice sessions are most productive when we use the resource of inclusive attention. We translate notes on a page into effective motions that make tone production

Our practice sessions are most productive when we use the resource of inclusive attention.

possible, all the while staying in touch with our emotional responses to the music and the moment. If we need to give a little more attention to something—bringing a note in tune, or finding balance over the floor—we can do this without losing sight of the whole by simply bringing it into the central circle for the moment.

Planes of Perception

Once I began studying Body Mapping, my oboe teaching changed. No longer could I just work on notes and reed-making with students. I now help students fully embody their performances. I have discovered that oboe students tend to think of their bodies as divided into six different planes: front, back, upper half, lower half (legs), right and left sides. They have certain unconscious prejudices about these areas of the body.

Oboe players pay a lot of attention to things up front. They hold the oboe in front of them. Most oboe training emphasizes things in the front, such as fingerings, embouchure positions, articulation at the reed, and even some abdominal movements. Many oboe players also think of taking in air as something that only happens in the front. Oboe players rarely pay attention to things in the back at all.

Oboists pay attention to their upper half more than their legs. Notice that the things we pay attention to in the front of the body are all part of the upper body as well. Oboe players rarely notice their legs and feet while performing.

Oboists tend to associate the right hand with the lower part of the instrument, and the left hand with the upper part of the instrument. Many players favor one hand over the other, usually favoring that side of the body over the other, too.

Some people speak of oboists as being "symmetrical" when compared to other instrumentalists, particularly flutists and violinists. It's true that these "asymmetrical" instrumentalists have special issues because they constantly hold the instrument to one side. And these issues can have debilitating side effects (pardon the pun), such as neck pain, rotator cuff syndrome, or tendonitis. But I've observed that oboe and English horn players can develop problems that are equally debilitating because of their often-unconscious prejudices toward inequality: favoring front over back, upper over lower, right over left. When these unconscious prejudices are brought into awareness, the path to recovery has already begun.

Embodying oboe performance means the mind works with the whole body to bring out the best possible musical performance. To make this happen, we must consciously find ways to bring the whole body into our awareness as we play.

Agenda Helper **1**

Oboemotions

The Agenda Helper is a means for determining the direction of your practice for the week. Read the statements and put a check mark by those that are true for you. The statements you leave blank indicate where your training should be directed.

It's useful to return to the Agenda Helper many times. Wouldn't it be wonderful if your practicing and study of Body Mapping brings you to the point where all of these statements are true?

- ❑ I clearly perceive my emotions when I play.
- ❑ I clearly perceive my motions when I play.
- ❑ My body map is accurate.
- ❑ My body map is adequate.
- ❑ I perceive my position clearly as I play.
- ❑ I play at full stature, neither stretched nor compressed.
- ❑ I clearly perceive the quality of my own movement as I play.
- ❑ I clearly perceive when I am tense.
- ❑ I can readily free myself when I am tense.
- ❑ I clearly perceive when I am off balance.
- ❑ I can readily bring myself back to balance when I am off balance.
- ❑ I feel supported as I play.
- ❑ If I begin to lose support as I play, I can readily get it back.
- ❑ I use appropriate effort when I play.
- ❑ I have a clear intention as I play, and I carry out my intention.
- ❑ If I begin to use excess effort when I play, I can readily return to appropriate effort.
- ❑ I play without pain.
- ❑ I play without injury.
- ❑ I play with such integrity that I am not vulnerable to pain or injury.
- ❑ I am awake tactilely as I play.
- ❑ I am awake kinesthetically as I play.
- ❑ I clearly perceive my sensations as I play.
- ❑ I use my sensations as information when I play.
- ❑ I know what to do with the information I am receiving from my body as I play.
- ❑ I am kinesthetically sensitive as I play.
- ❑ I have a good quality of attention when I play, neither concentrated nor scanning.
- ❑ I am self-perceiving and world-perceiving as I play.

Chapter 3

Balance: Standing, Sitting, and Developing a Whole Body Awareness

People need to map themselves as vertebrates, "with everything related to the spine: head resting on it, arm structure hovering over it, and the pelvis and legs delivering their weight to the floor. Then we are not just a collection of parts but an organized collection of parts, with the spine serving its function as the organizing element."

Barbara Conable[5]

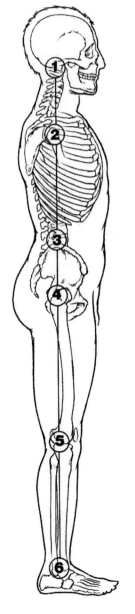

Sarah sat down for her first lesson and explained she had trouble moving her fingers quickly. She loved playing slow, expressive solos on the oboe, but when it came to playing fast passagework her fingers became unruly, moving unevenly or locking up. She had tried other teachers' suggestions to practice with a metronome, change rhythms, etc. Even though things improved, she felt her playing lacked the fluidity she heard in other oboe players.

I asked her to play something for me that she was having trouble with. As she played Vivaldi, I noticed her head. It was pulled forward and down. She rocked nervously from side to side and appeared ill at ease in the chair. I interrupted and asked, "Do you mostly practice sitting or standing?" She paused for a second, then started laughing nervously. "Sometimes I practice sitting down and sometimes I practice standing up. The thing is, I really don't know how to sit or stand!" she exclaimed.

Now I laughed, too. Of course, Sarah knew how to sit and stand—she's been doing these things since she was a toddler. But the point was that she was very uncomfortable with sitting and standing, even though these are activities she does for a large part of the day, every day.

There are many performers like Sarah. Feeling uncomfortable with sitting and standing is often a signal that your body is off-balance in relation to the chair or floor. This loss of balance can limit many movements that help us as oboe players: not just the finger movements Sarah noticed she had trouble with, but also

15

arm movements needed to hold and move the instrument; leg movements needed to maintain balance; and especially the many movements needed for tension-free breathing. When students who don't feel comfortable with sitting and standing are helped, they experience a relief that seems to improve confidence and the ability to focus. Someone who feels one hundred percent confident about sitting and standing finds it much easier to freely and gracefully maneuver the many and varied movements performers require.

Feeling uncomfortable with sitting and standing is often a signal that your body is off-balance in relation to the chair or floor.

We each develop habits for sitting and standing, and these habitual actions have been well established long before any of us start to play the oboe. So even though double reed players tend to be inquisitive people (How do you make a reed? How do you tongue faster? How do you play loud? How do you get to Carnegie Hall?), we rarely think to ask, "How do you stand better?" Those that do ask are often given answers that aren't really specific enough to help. "Stand straight!" or "Be more relaxed!" they are told. In many cases these injunctions do more harm than good. There are some people who have developed habitual ways of sitting and standing which are well coordinated and feel buoyant. But many others are like Sarah. They have developed ways of sitting and standing that do not support good oboe playing.

Some habits, like sitting and standing, can be so ingrained that one doesn't realize how limiting they are; in fact, one may not even realize they exist. People with these sorts of ingrained habits must increase their kinesthetic awareness and make a conscious effort to become more observant of the habitual movement patterns they have developed. Then they must realize the potential the mind has to work with the body. The mind/body connection can create new patterns of movement that support better balance. Body Mapping is a powerful tool for increasing awareness and gaining conscious control over habitual actions.

For Sarah, not knowing how to stand or sit prevented her from moving her fingers freely. As she learned how to maintain good balance while standing or sitting, the tension that restricted her fingers was released and her playing improved.

The Posture and Relaxation Clubs

Oboe players who are not comfortable with their sitting or standing usually belong to one of two opposing "clubs": either the "good posture" club, or the "relaxation" club. The members of the good posture club hold themselves up, looking somewhat rigid with chest high and shoulders back. The small of the back may be overarched. When they are standing, their knees will often be locked. Members of this club may have once had a teacher who lined students up against a wall in order to instill this notion of "good" posture.

Members of the relaxation club may feel relaxed, but they often appear uninvolved. They sit toward the back of a chair, slightly slumped, with head forward, shoulders and chest compressed down. Or they may sit with hips toward the front of the chair and torso leaned back, resting their upper back against the back of the chair, with neck pulled forward to reach the oboe. Though they call this relaxed, in fact, their muscles are working hard to create and maintain this position. Membership in either club interferes with good oboe playing.

What should good balance look like? Athletes are excellent models for balance. Watch a great baseball player walk toward the plate and then assume the batting position. Legs are grounded, torso is poised over the legs in a manner that supports the arms. The arms are capable at any moment of swinging at a variety of angles and speeds with great control. Think of the tennis player with arms outstretched to release a serve, or a boxer, feet in constant motion, head and torso bobbing in anticipation of a blow. The positions these athletes must assume for their goals are quite different from each other. Yet all outstanding athletes exhibit naturalness and a liveliness that allows them to follow through with the task at hand. Musicians who are comfortable with sitting and standing will exhibit this same naturalness and lively awareness.

Oboe players should not think there is just one position for great oboe playing. Finding the right balance for sitting or standing while playing an instrument requires the performer to develop a kinesthetic awareness of joints and muscles. In this chapter you will learn how mapping joints such as the A-O joint, the hip, knee, and ankle can bring you greater muscular freedom. This increased understanding of the relationship of these joints to each other will allow you to find greater comfort in standing and sitting.

It is common for teachers to observe a student slumping, and then ask them to "sit up straight." The student's usual response to this is rigidity. Or the teacher sees a student standing rigidly and asks them to "relax." Now the student begins slumping! For teachers to get what they're after, they should help students cultivate beautiful balance and kinesthetic awareness. Finding good balance is not really about how someone looks on the outside. Improved awareness of one's internal structure, including the function and size of bones at joints, results in more expressive and accurate performance.

The A-O Joint

Like so many of my colleagues, I've had to travel a lot in order to pursue a musical career. When relocating to a new city, one of the first things I do is purchase an atlas so I can easily find my way to gigs! Well, it turns out we have an atlas inside our bodies. The top vertebra of the spine is named the *atlas*. It is the balancing point for our skull. Just as reading an atlas will help me find my way around a new city, becoming familiar with the atlas at the top of the spine is the key to finding balance throughout the body.

Accurately mapping the atlas is crucial to good wind playing. So let's take time to locate it and better understand its structure and function.

The atlas derives its name from the Greek myth about Atlas, the Titan condemned to hold up the heavens with his shoulders. Like this mythological being, the atlas at the top of our spine supports a heavy weight—the head. Just as the top vertebra of the spine has been given a name, the atlas, the bottom part of the skull resting on top of the atlas has a name, too: the *occiput*. The joint where the atlas and occiput meet is called the atlanto-occipital joint, or more simply, the A-O joint.

The atlas is at the top of your neck and almost as wide as this part of the body, providing enough surface area to balance the head. There are two slight depressions on the bony surface of the atlas called the facets. The bottom of the skull has two slight protrusions, called condyles, that fit readily into the facets of the atlas. This relationship of atlas to occiput provides for easy movement as well as secure balance.

Accurately mapping the atlas is crucial to good wind playing.

Look at figures 3.1–2 to see exactly where the A-O joint is located. Although this joint can't be seen from the outside, it can be felt from the inside because it is loaded with sense receptors. Take time to develop a kinesthetic sense of precisely where your skull rocks on the atlas. You will feel it right in the center of your head, between your ears.

When you play the oboe, the reed is pointing directly at the A-O joint! Think of all the other things happening near this joint. The brain is right above it, monitoring bodily functions as well as all of the emotional and intellectual aspects of music making. The eyes are above and in front of it, receiving

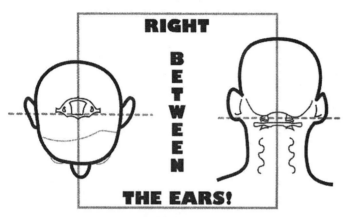

Figure 3.1.

information from the score and transmitting it to the brain. Directly in front of the A-O joint are the openings through which we inhale and exhale: the nose and mouth. The trachea, or windpipe, is below it in the front, providing a passageway for air to and from the lungs. The tongue and soft palate are also just in front of this joint, helping to alter reed vibrations and shape the sounds we hear with our ears. The ears are located on both sides of the A-O joint.

Find Your A-O Joint

Notice any tension in your neck. If there is muscular tension, then ask your neck muscles to release. Place your thumb on your ear. Place your fingers on the base of your skull. Begin gently nodding, noticing how this movement occurs at a joint right between your ears.

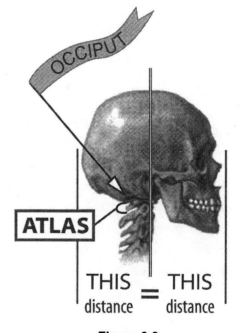

Figure 3.2.

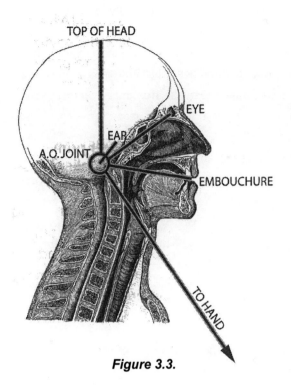

Figure 3.3.

There are many mis-mappings of the A-O joint that can create problems for oboe players. Some map the balance of the skull to the back of the neck instead of in the center of the head. This pulls the head back, creating unnecessary tension in both the front and back of the neck. It is also common to mis-map the connection of skull to spine much lower than it actually is. Some map the balance of the head approximately where the top of a shirt collar would be. Take time to nod your head from this point of your neck. Really notice the quality of this movement, the amount of effort it takes. Now nod your head from the actual position of the A-O joint, and notice what's different about this movement.

Mapping the A-O joint accurately releases excess tension in the neck and throughout the body. It can make breathing easier.

Mapping the A-O joint accurately has many positive results. It releases excess tension in the neck and throughout the body. It can make one feel taller and breathe easier.

To more fully appreciate the importance of the A-O joint, we must look at what lies directly below— the rest of the spine.

The Spine

Many oboists complain about reeds. And it's easy to understand why. A bad reed has dire consequences—the tone quality can be unfocused or overly strident, intonation can be wildly sharp or flat, notes won't speak when or how you want them to. One of the tricks to scraping a good reed is understanding how to "balance" the reed—using the knife to scrape one side of the blade of cane in a way that mirrors the other. When we make a well-balanced reed, we describe the reed as "stable" and find that it allows us to play with a focused tone, good intonation, and good response.

Just like the reed, the body must be well balanced in order to feel stable. A performer who is not balanced in relation to the floor (or the chair) experiences many of the same

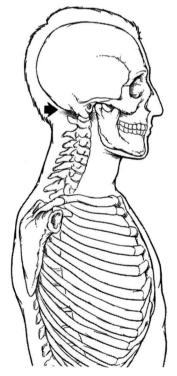

Figure 3.4.

19

problems one experiences with an unbalanced reed—un-centered tone, faulty intonation, and unreliable articulations.

A well-balanced oboe reed has a spine. This spine is at the center of the reed and helps provide stability. The spine in our body shares these qualities with the spine of an oboe reed. Our spine helps us find balance and stability and is central to the body.

You may be wondering, "How is the spine central to the body?" Many imagine that the spine is at the back of the body. In fact, another word for spine is backbone. You can feel bony protrusions all along your back to confirm that there is, in fact, spine at the back. However, this part of the spine, the part you can palpate, is only part of the story. Much of the spine is at the center of your body, and the centrality of the spine allows for good balance and good movement. Understanding the whole story of the spine—its structure, function and size—is another important key toward finding and maintaining balance.

It's time to more closely inspect the reality of the spine.

The spine's architecture beautifully integrates form and function. Its form is ideal for the function of bearing and delivering weight. Looking at the spine one immediately sees that it is not straight. It is curved in an S shape. The curved structure of the spine gives it a greater capacity to absorb impact. One also notices that the spine is segmented. It is made up of many individual vertebrae separated by intervertebral disks. This arrangement gives the spine a tremendous flexibility, making the curved structure possible and also allowing for a wide variety of movements.

As we look more closely at the spine, we see that there is a front and back to it. In the middle is a passage for the spinal cord with room for the many nerves which connect to the spinal cord. The bony structure of the spine serves to protect this all-important system that directly connects the brain to the rest of the body.

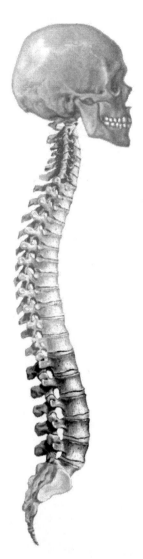

Figure 3.5. *Three regions of the spine*

The back of the spine looks quite different from the front. It has bony protrusions that remind one of the dinosaur, the stegosaurus. These are the bony parts that you can palpate along your back. This structure also accommodates their function, serving as points of attachment for muscles and ligaments.

Notice that the intervertebral disks do not exist in the back of the spine. Movement between the vertebrae is more limited in the back because of the stegosaurus-like structure, and weight is not distributed easily through the back because of the lack of cushioning disks. The disks in the front of the spine act as shock absorbers, cushioning bones from the effects of walking, jumping, and other similar activities. The disks are filled with a gelatinous material that allows for movement between the vertebrae. Because of this, the spine itself has the ability to gather and lengthen in support of breathing and other movements.

To sum up:

The spine's structure:
> Curved and segmented with a front portion separated by disks, a middle cavity, and a back portion with spiky protrusions.

The spine's function:
> It moves, absorbs shock, houses the spinal cord, provides attachments for muscles, and bears and delivers weight.

The spine is often described as being divided in three sections. These three sections also relate to both structure and function. The bottom, forward-facing curve of the spine's S structure is called the *lumbar* spine. It consists of the bottom five vertebrae. This part of the spine connects to the pelvis. The middle twelve vertebrae, making up the back-facing middle curve of the spine, are called the *thoracic* spine. Connected to these twelve vertebrae are twelve ribs on the left and twelve on the right side of the body. The top part of the spine is curved, forward-facing (like the lumbar spine) and consists of seven vertebrae. It is called the *cervical* spine.

When the whole spine is well aligned, its design fully supports the weight of the head. The head seesaws at its fulcrum over a well-aligned spine, moving easily forward as in nodding yes, and moving easily upward as in playing to the third balcony.

Until we release tension in the neck, it is difficult or impossible to release it elsewhere.

The head weighs between eight and twelve pounds, about the same as a bowling ball. But the spine's structure allows it to easily support this weight. If the head is balanced over the A-O joint, the neck muscles are free of tension. But if the head is forward of the A-O joint or pulled too far back, then neck muscles tense to compensate for this imbalance.

Muscular tension in the neck has a ripple effect, creating tension in other muscles below the neck. Until we release tension in the neck, it is difficult or impossible to release it elsewhere. For oboe players, poor alignment inhibits the muscular freedom needed to breathe easily and have flexible embouchures, reactive tongues, buoyant arms, and free fingers. This is the reason it is so important for oboists to develop kinesthetic awareness of the A-O joint as well as an awareness of neck freedom when playing.

FREE   TIGHT

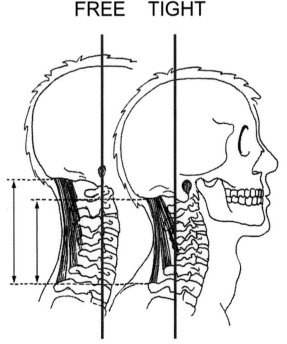

Figure 3.6. *Comparison of free and tight necks*

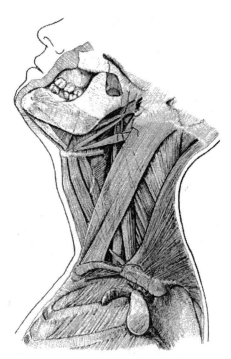

Figure 3.7. *Layers of neck muscles*

In order to free the neck muscles, you should get acquainted with them. This is because much neck tension is the direct result of mis-mapping the neck in important ways. Be sure you carefully compare what you learn here about the structure of the neck with your own map so that you can easily correct any mis-mapping you may have. There are many layers of neck muscles, superficial and deep, which serve many different movement functions. Some of them are shown in figure 3.7.

Our bodies are organized around a central core. The A-O joint aligned over the lumbar spine is a major part of this vertical core running through the center of our bodies. Some compare the A-O joint to the fulcrum of a seesaw. Oboists who belong to the posture club tend to hold the weight of the head behind the fulcrum; those who belong to the relaxation club bring the weight of the head forward of the fulcrum. Either way the seesaw is off balance, and the side with the heavier weight is pulled back and down. When the head is balanced directly over the fulcrum, its weight is transferred directly to the atlas. This allows the head to move forward and up. It feels weightless.

A Note for English Horn Players

Some English horn players want to tilt the head downward slightly so that the angle of the reed feels comfortable against the embouchure. One should accomplish this by paying utmost attention to maintaining free neck muscles, with the head well balanced over the A-O joint. If you find yourself wanting to tilt the head forward and down, away from balance, then experiment with other means of adjusting the reed angle: either use the arms to move the instrument into a different position or a different bocal with a more agreeable angle.

Lumbar Spine (Watch Your Back!)

The bottom five vertebrae of the spine comprise the lumbar region. They are the largest vertebrae and provide support for the head, thorax, and arms above them. The front weight-bearing part of the lumbar region curves forward to a central position in the body. Similar to the way one finds balance at the A-O joint, one needs to find balance in the lumbar spine, too.

Watch your back! Many musicians throw the weight of the upper body onto their backs, creating chronic tension in lower back muscles. Instead, gently shift the weight forward onto the lumbar spine to find balance in sitting and standing as well as relief from back pain.

Pelvis: Rockers and Hip Joints

Understanding the pelvis and the role it plays in balance and weight delivery is every bit as important as understanding the neck. The spine begins in the neck at the A-O joint, the critical juncture where the head finds its balance. The spine ends in the pelvis. The important job of weight bearing and weight delivery that the spine so beautifully fulfills must now be transferred to some other part of the body.

The pelvis is where this weight transfer occurs. Figure 3.9 clearly shows where the spine connects: at the sacrum. Two other important features of the pelvis are the rockers (sit bones, or ischial tuberosities) and hip joints. You want to become very aware of the precise location of these places in your body. Understanding the structure, function, and size of your rockers and hip joints will help you find stability when sitting and standing.

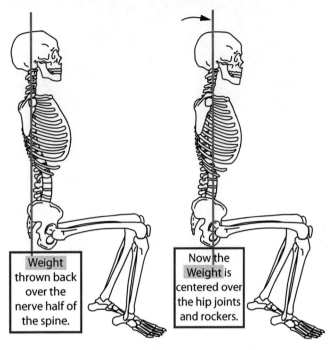

Weight thrown back over the nerve half of the spine.

Now the Weight is centered over the hip joints and rockers.

Figure 3.8. Balance while sitting

Find Your Rockers

Sitting on a hard chair, rock your pelvis forward and back, as well as side to side and feel how the sit bones make contact with the chair. To get a better sense of how weight is delivered through the rockers, place your hands, palms up, underneath them as you rock back and forth and side to side.

The rockers are the bottom of your torso.

Look at figure 3.8. Notice in the drawing on the right that weight is distributed from the bottom of the skull at the A-O joint all the way down through the rockers when sitting in balance. The drawing to the left shows off-balance sitting. This person's weight is directed toward the back, creating muscular tension in the neck as well as lower back, and making it feel uncomfortable when sitting.

When you find this balance on the rockers in sitting, then your legs will feel free to move. You won't feel as though you are sitting on your legs. When sitting, the thigh bones should get out of the way and let you balance on your rockers. The thigh bones are connected to the pelvis above the rockers and on your sides. The hip joint is the place on the outside of the pelvis where thigh bone meets pelvis. Knowing precisely where the hip joints are located can help oboe players with many things they must do: sitting, standing, and taking a bow!

The weight of your torso is delivered outward through the hip joints to the thigh bones when you are standing or squatting. Figure 3.9 shows that the pelvis and thigh bones form an arch structure. This bony architecture is able to bear weight easily, providing tremendous stability.

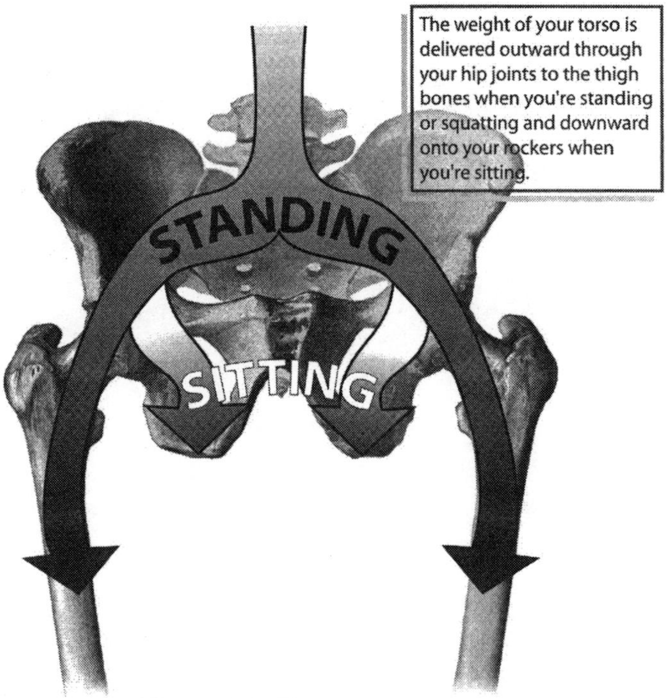

The weight of your torso is delivered outward through your hip joints to the thigh bones when you're standing or squatting and downward onto your rockers when you're sitting.

STANDING

SITTING

Figure 3.9. *The arch of the pelvis*

In standing, weight is delivered from the lumbar spine through the thickened part of the sacrum sideways through the sacroiliac joints to the thickened part of the pelvic bone into the hip joints and through the hip joints to the upper thigh bone to the shaft and downward to the floor. In sitting, weight is delivered through a smaller arch to the chair by means of the sitting bones.

Find Your Hip Joints

While standing, use your hands to get a sense of where your hip joints are. When asked to point to the hip joint, many will instead point to the top of the pelvis. This spot (the iliac crest) is a bony arch on your sides that is easily palpated. Find your iliac crests with your hands. March in place and notice that you do not feel leg movement where your hands are. Now move your hands down your sides until you feel the bones that are at the top of your legs. This portion of the thighbone, clearly seen in figure 3.10, is called the greater *trochanter.* The hip joint is inward and upward from the greater trochanter.

The hip joint is the halfway point of the body. The torso makes up the upper half, the legs the lower half. Many believe the waist is the midpoint. But as we learn more about the reality of the body's structure, we discover that bodies actually don't have waists. This discovery is actually quite a relief to many people! Clothes have waistlines, but bodies don't.

Some use what is commonly thought of as a waist to initiate many simple activities, such as getting into and out of a chair, leaning back, or bowing at the end of a performance. All of these activities are accomplished with increased efficiency when initiated from the hip joints instead. Balance at the hip joints allows free movement of the torso as well as free movement of the legs.

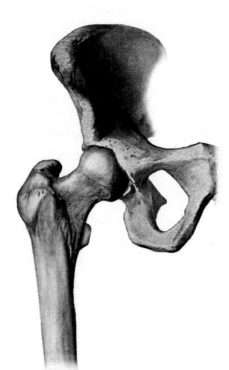

Figure 3.10. *The hip joint*

Legs

We have six leg joints—three for each leg. The first is the hip joint described above; the other two are at the knee and ankle. Familiarity with these joints helps us to find free legs which make us feel grounded when standing. Tense legs feel planted. We want to find balance between the leg joints in order to support the balance we've found in the torso.

Balance at the hip joints allows free movement of the torso as well as free movement of the legs.

As you find balance over your bony core, the many muscles of the legs will release tension and find freedom. Figure 3.12 shows that the muscles over the back of the pelvis, the *gluteus maximus* (and called many more colorful names in the vernacular), wrap around the pelvic bones from the tailbone to the hip joint, and are (through connective tissue) continuous with the muscles that spiral from the hip joint to the knee. When the glutes tighten, so do the thigh and calf muscles as well as the feet. Correctly mapping the pelvic arch and locating the hip joint will help free these muscles.

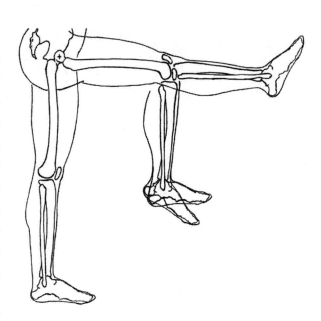

Figure 3.11. The six joints of the legs

Figure 3.12. Spirals of the leg

Understanding the knee joint is another way to recover free legs and find balance while standing. The knee joint is where the thigh and the lower leg meet. It is not the kneecap, which is located above and in front of the knee joint.

Knees can be locked, balanced, or bent. If the torso is not balanced, often the knees will lock. This is the body's way of protecting the lower back when one goes off-balance. Knee locking can be momentary, with the knees returning to balance as the body does. But chronic knee locking inhibits free movement and makes it impossible to find balance over the floor. Consistently locking the knees is an indication that balance has not been found above the knee. When you find balance in the upper body—at the A-O joint, lumbar spine, and hip joints—the knees will unlock.

The ankle joint is where the lower leg meets the foot. The lower leg has two bones, the *tibia* and *fibula*. The two bumps that you can feel near the ankle are the bottom of these

25

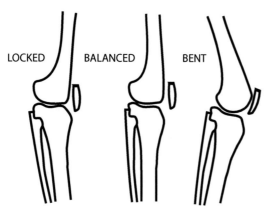

Figure 3.13. Three states of the knee

two bones. These bumps are not your ankle joint (as many players have mapped it). Your ankle joint lies just below and in front of them.

Oboists can move in subtle ways at the ankle joints in order to maintain balance over the floor. In balanced standing, weight is distributed equally toward the front and back of the foot. The body's weight is delivered through the front of the leg (tibia, or shinbone) to the center of the arch of the foot. This arch delivers the weight equally toward the back at the heel and the front across the spreading ball of the foot. The toes are not part of the arch, so they should be able to wiggle freely.

Some mis-map the body's weight as delivered through the back of the leg into the heel of the foot, thereby locking their legs and off-balancing to the back. The ankle, however, is not L-shaped. One can find balance by correctly mapping the ankle joint to the foot.

Find Your Balance

Notice the way you deliver weight to the floor when you stand. If you are gripping with your toes, then perhaps you have shifted the balance too far forward. If you are a member of the posture club, then you will feel the weight firmly in your heels. Find freedom in your neck and lower back. Gently move your body forward and back as you stand. Notice tension returning to your muscles as you deliver weight toward the toes, and then into the heels. You will experience freedom and balance when you are delivering the weight through the ankle joint to the central arch of the foot.

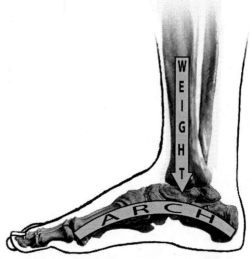

Figure 3.14. Weight delivery through the arch of the foot

Take care that the shoes you wear do not inhibit finding balance through the central arches of the feet. Wear shoes that fit properly. If you are flat-footed, then wear an arch support. High-heeled shoes should be carefully chosen; you can find fashionable shoes that still support good balance over the floor.

Summary: Points of Balance

The bony structure of the body is organized around a central vertical core. By developing a kinesthetic awareness of points along the core, we can consciously monitor good alignment. When the body's skeletal structure is well aligned, it holds us upright, bears the body's weight and delivers it to the floor or chair. Our muscles are then free to act and react in response to messages from the brain.

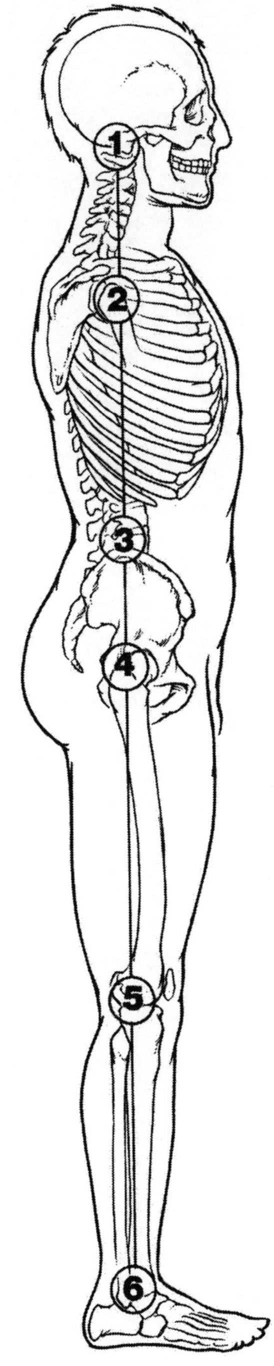

This chapter examines several key points along the body's central core: the A-O joint, the lumbar spine, and the hip, knee, and ankle joints. For oboe players to feel comfortable sitting and standing they need to become as familiar with these key points as they are with major and minor scales.

Musicians are trained to hear the pitch they are playing, determine if it is flat or sharp, and then make an adjustment to bring it in tune. They can also be trained to notice if they are standing or sitting in a well-balanced manner. When we are not in balance, we can learn to bring ourselves back to balance just as easily as bringing a note in tune.

> When we are not in balance, we can learn to bring ourselves back to balance just as easily as bringing a note in tune.

One other structure of the body that helps us monitor for good balance around the central core is the arm. Arms have so many other ways of impacting our performance that I've devoted a whole chapter just to them. With an understanding of how a whole body works with the mind to create and undo basic postural habits, we can now tackle the F. E. A. T. of oboe playing. The next few chapters look at the most basic aspects of oboe playing—fingers, embouchure, air, and tongue—in the context of a whole body.

Figure 3.15. Six points of balance

Chapter 4
Applying Alexander's Orders

Teachers of the Alexander Technique often use Alexander's orders to help pupils find freedom and ease in their movements. These orders are not meant as commandments that students must make happen. F. M. Alexander realized that the mind/body bond was so strong that merely the suggestion of something by the mind could immediately have an effect on the body. We don't force an action, we don't try to "do" anything. Instead we just observe, allowing the body its natural response.

Alexander's orders are:

1. I will allow my neck [muscles] to be free,
2. so that my head will go forward and up,
3. so that my back will lengthen and widen.

This Alexander Technique strategy of using orders has been very helpful to many musicians, which is why I mention them here. Though *Oboemotions* is not an Alexander Technique book, it is about establishing beautiful balance and freeing muscles by means of correcting and refining the body map. I recommend these orders as a means of clarifying and carrying out your intentions. Get very comfortable carrying out the orders on yourself before attempting to incorporate them into your practice routine.

Using Sensory Imagination

The exercise in figure 4.1 uses imagery in a variety of sophisticated ways. You must imagine the sound of the music before you play it—not just the emotion and phrasing, but also the quality of the tone, with dynamics and perfect intonation. You must recite orders and use kinesthesia to notice if these orders have an effect on your body. You are asked to mentally picture alignment at the A-O joint, lumbar spine, hip, knee, and ankle joints. You are invited to do all of these at one time.

We work with objective representations for these subjective experiences—notes on a staff, words on a page, artists' renderings of the human body. Musicians may already be comfortable with imagining the notes on a page. We translate the visual imagery of those notes into powerful and heartfelt performances. Many of us also use our aural imagination, "hearing" a concerto from start to finish in our heads. Often this imagined performance will improve our actual performance.

Most musicians I know have pretty active imaginations. When practicing, we can use imagination for more than just hearing notes. Kinesthetic and visual imagination are just as useful for musicians as aural imagination. It's been proven that when athletes train themselves to visualize their movements, their performance improves. As musicians better understand how movement is responsible for every aspect of performance, they develop similar sensory skills. As we study illustrations of how the body is put together and take time to explore how our own bodies are put together, we will imagine beautiful music linked to free and efficient movements.

Body Mapping Practice 1

Balance

Use the exercise in figure 4.1 below or substitute any similar warm-up exercise.

1. Practice from a standing position.
2. Before you play the exercise, take time to notice yourself as you repeat Alexander's orders.
3. As you play, continue to notice your balance. Free the neck muscles, release the head forward and up, lengthen and widen through the back and legs, sense weight being delivered through the central arch of the foot to the floor.
4. Play every note with the most beautiful resonance you can find.
5. Listen to what happens between notes. The timbre of the adjacent notes should match as evenly as possible, creating a seamless legato.

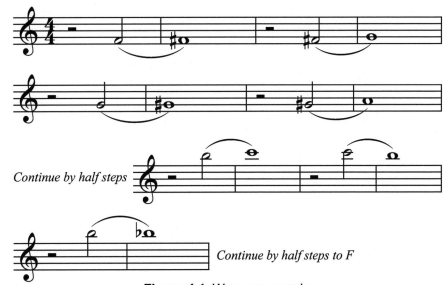

Figure 4.1. Warm-up exercise

Did you get through the whole exercise, maintaining an awareness of both beautiful music making as well as beautiful balance? If not, you can use a timer to help you.

1. Set the timer for thirty seconds.
2. Begin playing.
3. When the timer goes off, do you still have an awareness of balance?
4. If you do, then set it for forty-five seconds next time.
5. If you don't, then set the timer for fifteen seconds.
6. Eventually you want to play the whole warm-up with full inclusive attention.

There are numerous variations. Every day you can try a different one:

1. Play the exercise once, thinking mainly of freeing the neck muscles (which will release the head forward and up).
2. Now play it again, freeing the neck muscles *and* lengthening and widening through the back.
3. Practice at a *mezzo-forte* dynamic, then at *forte*, and then *piano*.
4. Try playing in a squat position.
5. It's helpful to practice with a mirror or a set of mirrors. It's also useful to videotape yourself as you play.
6. If you have discovered a problem with your body map, begin the work of correcting it as you play this music. In other words, if you are not sure about the central balance of the head over the A-O joint, then study figures 3.1–4 before playing the excerpt.
7. Keep these figures on your music stand as you play through the excerpt to continually remind you of this balance point.
8. You should also practice while sitting.

Chapter 5

Case Study Number 1: Martin Finds Balance

Martin approached me with a tentative smile and shook my hand. "I'm playing for you in the master class today." He stood with confidence. I noticed slight tension in his upper back and neck, but nothing out of the ordinary. Perhaps he was just a bit nervous about playing for me. Normal.

However, once he started playing, his body took a completely different form. His head came forward and down as he met the oboe and began playing the Mozart *Concerto*. It was a classic example of tense and contracted slumping, what F. M. Alexander described as "downward pull." In addition, it seemed to me that all his energy was focused on the area from his neck up. This area seemed completely disconnected from the rest of his body. This is not at all how he appeared when he shook hands with me, an act he achieved somewhat more naturally, using his whole body—his eyes looking at me, his hand extended, his body slightly forward. However, this natural connection to his whole self was lost when he played the oboe.

Despite the deficits I noticed in the physical aspect of his performance, the actual music making was quite good. He played with a small, but quite pretty sound and gave a mostly accurate and stylistic performance of the Mozart. There were, however, a couple of passages where fingers and tongue were not well-coordinated. There were also places where his breathing appeared labored.

I wanted to find out what Martin thought about his performance, so I complimented him on the nice things I heard him doing, then asked, "What do you feel is the most difficult thing about playing this piece?" He thought for a minute, then responded that it bothered him that often he would make little note mistakes (the finger/tongue coordination I had noticed). I asked him if it was possible that there was a physical reason this was happening. Had he noticed if there was anything he was doing physically when he went to play these passages that might be getting in the way? He answered that his neck gets tight when he's about to play those passages. "Sometimes it hurts a little." I next asked him how he went about practicing these passages to try to fix them.

"I play them slowly," Martin offered.

"Does your neck feel tight when you play slowly?" I asked.

"Yes."

I was a little surprised that he noticed pain even when he practiced slowly, yet he had never tried to release this pain. I gave him two prescriptions. First I helped him correct his body map, because a mis-mapping of the relationship of the head to the spine was the source of his problem. Then I gave him a method for practicing that would allow him to incorporate the new mapping into his everyday experience of playing the oboe.

I reminded him of the crucial balance of the spine and the skull at the A-O joint. Martin did not have an accurate map of where this balance occurs and how it functions. I showed him that it was in the middle of his head. I described it like a seesaw. Just as two people on each end of the seesaw can make it move up and down, the weight of the front and back parts of the skull compete to pull us off balance, either pulling us down or bringing us too far back. I asked Martin to experiment for himself with this natural balance.

"First allow the weight of the front part of the skull to bring you forward. Notice how this feels on your neck, back, legs. Then let the back part of the skull pull you back. This also has an effect on your neck and other parts of your body. Where do you notice tension? Now find the natural balance of the skull and spine. It's a place where the tensions of the other two positions are released and the head is held up effortlessly."

"When you played the Mozart *Concerto* you played very well in tune. So I know that you've already developed your hearing to a very refined level. You can discriminate if a pitch is flat or sharp and fix it immediately. You can use this same ability to get better 'in tune' with your body as you play."

I asked Martin to bring his head off-balance again in the "downward pull" position. I told him to think of this as "flat." I then asked him to go off-balance in the opposite direction—head back. "This is sharp."

"As you play, just as you notice pitch and correct it, now add to your awareness the discrimination of the balance of your skull on the spine. If you notice yourself going off-balance, fix it, just like you would fix the high C at the beginning of the Mozart *Concerto* if you notice it's out of tune."

Now I had Martin pick up the oboe again. I introduced him to Alexander's orders as a means of incorporating good balance into his daily routine. "Free your neck muscles so that your head goes forward and up and your back lengthens and widens." Martin did a nice job of following the orders, finding a relatively good sense of overall balance. However, just before he went to play the oboe again, he moved the neck slightly forward, bringing him back to the "downward pull" he was comfortable with. Yes, he was comfortable with something that gave him discomfort! The downward pull wasn't as extreme as his usual habit, and his playing did sound better. I asked him how he felt about his playing and he said it felt and sounded better.

"Did you notice that just before you played, your neck moved forward?"

" No," Martin answered. In fact, he didn't believe me when I said that it had moved.

So I had him play again. I went through Alexander's orders one more time. Again he got himself nicely aligned, and again just before playing he moved off-balance. But this time he noticed he did it. A-ha.

So I guided him through the process one more time. Now Martin began playing from a place of balance. The tone was much richer. The fingers and tongue moved effortlessly. We all noticed a difference and the audience at the master class applauded encouragingly.

Agenda Helper **2**

Balance

Mark the statements that are true for you. Work on the ones that aren't checked.

❑ I feel balance when I play.

❑ I am neither slumped nor "postury" as I play.

❑ I feel springy and poised when I play.

❑ My map of my spine is accurate.

❑ My head is dynamically poised on my spine when I play.

❑ My thorax is dynamically poised on my lumbar vertebrae as I play.

❑ My upper half is dynamically poised on my legs as I play.

❑ I am dynamically poised at my knees as I play.

❑ I am dynamically poised at my ankles as I play.

❑ My arm structure is dynamically poised over my torso and legs as I play.

❑ I can readily move in any direction from balance as I play.

❑ There is no waist in my body map.

❑ I know my hip joints and pelvic floor are my middle, and I am dynamically poised over my legs as I play.

❑ I feel very stable, poised over my legs as I stand.

❑ I know right where my hip joints are.

❑ I move my legs without tension in my inner thighs.

❑ I have full range of motion at my hip joints.

❑ I move my legs without tension in my lower back.

❑ My gluteus muscles are free as I play.

❑ My hamstrings are free as I play.

❑ My calf muscles are free as I play.

❑ I feel grounded as I play.

❑ I use my ankles appropriately as I play.

❑ My legs are lively to me as I play.

❑ I perceive my legs clearly as I play.

❑ I never feel pain in my legs as I play.

❑ I never lock my knees when I play, except when I am gesturing backwards.

❑ I never play with chronically bent knees. I just return again and again to balance at my knees.

❑ I sit poised on my sitting bones as I play.

Chapter 6

Fingers

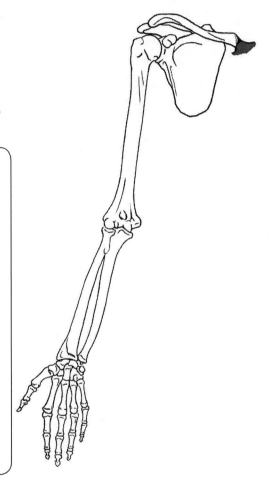

There is nothing remarkable about it. All one has to do is hit the right notes at the right time, and the instrument plays itself.

Johann Sebastian Bach,
responding to a compliment about his
remarkable organ playing.[6]

Note

Throughout this chapter there are references to specific keys on the oboe. This is meant to refer to the Semi-automatic Conservatory mechanism, the most commonly used oboe mechanism in the world. If you play one of the many other systems available (automatic, thumb plate, Viennese, or historical oboes) you will want to make adjustments accordingly. However, the bulk of information in this chapter should be useful for all oboists. No matter what type of instrument you play, you still use two arms and ten fingers to play it!

An oboist's hands have two jobs: maneuvering the keys and balancing the instrument. When we first learn to play the instrument, we really pay attention to our fingers. We struggle to get used to balancing the instrument, while remembering a variety of awkward-feeling fingering combinations. But soon it all becomes second nature and we hardly notice what we're doing anymore—until we run into trouble.

When we're confronted by technical passagework that seems too difficult for us, or when we feel pain, we reevaluate what we're doing with our arms. Unfortunately the arms are the most common source of pain for oboe players. For some these pains become injuries: tendonitis, tenosynovitis, carpal tunnel syndrome, torn ligaments, and tennis elbow (lateral epicondylitis) are some of the afflictions that affect oboe players.

Pain is often blamed on overuse. A change in one's playing, or a significant increase in the length or intensity of one's schedule can lead to strain or inflammation of muscles or tendons if one is not moving well during these times. Musicians who play with poor postural habits can, over time, develop similar overuse symptoms. There are many musicians, however, who play for many years, many hours a day, and never develop pain from playing. So perhaps it is not *over*use, but rather, *mis*use that causes pain in oboe players.

An oboist's hands have two jobs: maneuvering the keys and balancing the instrument.

Nerve compression is another source of pain for double reed players. The most common type is carpal tunnel syndrome. Finally, osteoarthritis is another cause of pain which tends to affect players as they age. Osteoarthritis is a degenerative disease. At present it cannot be cured. However, its effects can be minimized by better understanding the arms in relation to the instrument, and by making certain postural adjustments when necessary to keep pressure off the affected parts.

This chapter explains the arm's structure in detail. When oboe players develop a playing technique cognizant of the arm's structure and function, playing becomes easier and there is less chance of injury or pain. Chapter 3 discussed balancing the body, so let's first look at how the arms balance the oboe in relation to a balanced body.

Balancing an Oboe

There are three points of balance for the oboe:

1. The right thumb, which rests against the oboe and the thumb rest and which bears the weight of the instrument (around two pounds).
2. The left hand, including the left thumb which moves between the wood of the oboe and the octave key (or keys, for oboes with third-octave keys).
3. The embouchure, against which the reed rests.

None of the three is completely stable, but that's okay. Embouchures move. The left hand must move quite a lot. The right thumb seems the most stable, but it too will move slightly for certain fingering patterns.

Sometimes we think about "holding" the oboe, and we grip with the fingers, trying to stabilize the instrument in a rigid fashion. But the combination of these balance points gives the instrument stability while allowing for movement at each.

To be completely comfortable in holding the instrument, oboists must map all three moveable balance points. Many oboe players have mapped their thumbs holding the oboe, but forget to also rely on the lips and jaw for balance. Others only map the right thumb as holding the full weight of the instrument. It's true that the right thumb is responsible for carrying the weight of the oboe. The left hand, however, serves as a counterbalance. At all times at least one finger of the left hand is on a key. The left thumb moves quite a bit more than the right, and at times isn't even on the oboe, but when it is (either on the wood or the octave key), it does help stabilize the instrument. Some oboe players ignore the left thumb and allow it to float freely in the air, thus losing some of the security of this counterbalance. To achieve a more secure feeling of balance, whenever possible the left thumb should be on the wood of the oboe or on an octave key.

Ultimately, your whole body holds the oboe. Some tend to map only a thumb holding the instrument. These same persons would never imagine the branches of a tree just floating in the air without a trunk! Branches, of course, can only stay up in the air when they are attached to the tree. Once we acknowledge and actively engage the support of the legs and spine, the arms begin to feel weightless, as if they're floating in air. But first we must find the connection from thumbs to hands, hands to arms, then hands and arms to torso and legs.

Myth Buster
The thumb supports the instrument.

This myth is unfortunately sustained by commonly used terms such as "thumb rest" or "thumb supports." What has been the result of oboe and English horn players thinking that only a thumb supports the instrument? Far too many cases of pain, even injury, to hands and arms.

Myth Replacement
A whole arm supports the instrument. Arms feel supported when the body is in balance.

Understanding the Arm's Structure

Figure 6.1 shows a whole arm, which we use to hold oboes and English horns. It has four joints: the wrist, elbow, humero-scapular, and sterno-clavicular joints. The hand is attached to the lower arm at the wrist. The lower arm meets the upper arm at the elbow joint. Then there's the part often referred to as the shoulder. It's where the upper arm meets the shoulder blade and is called the humero-scapular joint. Finally, there's the joint that links the arm structure to the rest of our skeleton, the sterno-clavicular joint. Find each of these joints in figure 6.1. Refer to this figure as we explore each joint in more detail.

The only place where the arms directly connect to the bony foundation of the body is at the sterno-clavicular joints. This is where the collarbones (clavicles) meet the breastbone (sternum). Many don't acknowledge that the collarbones and the shoulder blades (scapulae) are part of the arms, but as you explore the variety of ways arms can move, you understand

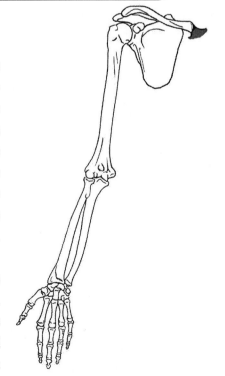

***Figure 6.1.** Four arm joints*

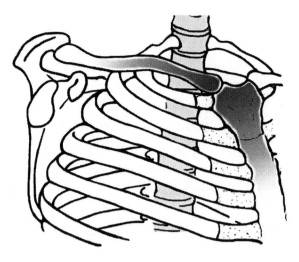

Figure 6.2. *The sterno-clavicular joint*

that collarbones and shoulder blades are essential to many of the arm's movements.

Playing the oboe doesn't require the range of arm movements that many other instruments need. Violinists shift from low notes on the g-string to notes near the bridge on the e-string, all the while performing intricate movements with the bow. Pianists make amazingly agile arm motions in order to produce great music from a keyboard. In comparison, oboists' arm movements appear quite limited, causing players to think arms are used only to hold the instrument.

Having this perception can lead some oboe players to "fix" the top of the arm structure. The collarbones and shoulder blades become locked, the oboist perhaps thinking this effort will better support holding the instrument. But in fact it has just the opposite effect. This locking not only keeps the whole arm from properly supporting the instrument, but also inhibits one from reaping the benefits of the primary support a balanced body offers. Equally unfortunate is the negative effect that locking the arm structure has on breathing.

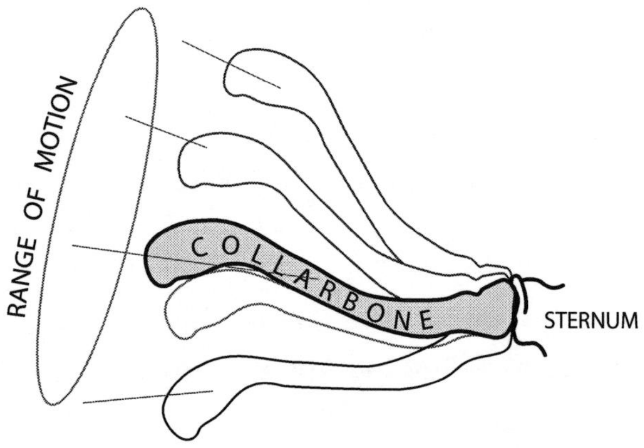

Even though we'll never need the range of motion at the clavicles that trombonists need, it is important for oboe players to have movement available at the sterno-clavicular joint in order to avoid locking the arms.

There is a lot of movement available at the sterno-clavicular joint.

Figure 6.3. *Movement at the sterno-clavicular joint*

Collarbones can move forward and back, up and down, and they can rotate.

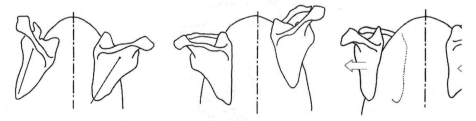

Figure 6.4. *Movement of scapula*

The shoulder blades are closely linked to the collarbone, and are responsive to their movements. Some map the shoulder blades as being directly attached to the ribs. They are not. They serve as shields, protecting the ribs and lungs, but are quite mobile, as seen in figure 6.4.

The second arm joint is where the humerus (upper arm bone) meets the scapula (shoulder blade). Some often mis-map the shoulder as a single thing. But one can see that this joint is

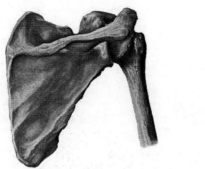

Figure 6.5. Humero-scapular joint

much more than a single thing—it is a ball-and-socket joint. The upper arm is the ball that fits into the socket of the scapula. The shoulder blade socket is small compared to the upper arm bone, which means that a great deal of movement is available at this joint.

In figure 6.6 we see the upper arm structure in relation to the torso. At the top of the picture you can see the back of the spine; on the bottom you see the sternum. Notice the collarbones and shoulder blades and how elegantly they rest over the ribs. The humero-scapular joints are located directly at the center of the body.

This central position of the arms at the humero-scapular joint is another point that helps us find balance. Remember the posture and relaxation clubs (see chapter 3). The arms of club members will not be balanced as seen in figure 6.6. Posture club members follow the dictum, "shoulders back, chest high," and have arms held back of center. Relaxation club members droop forward of center. When arms are balanced at the sides and center, the muscles controlling the arms can move more freely.

Figure 6.6 is extremely important for oboe players. So many oboe players "reach" for the oboe as they go to play it. They pull the arms forward as their head and neck pull down toward the reed. People who do this will not look like this figure, but will have arms pulled forward of center. This affects overall balance and limits rib movement, which will have an adverse effect on breathing.

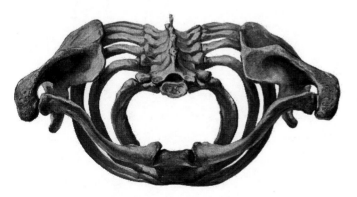

Figure 6.6. Arms over ribs

There are many important nerves and blood vessels passing between the collarbones and the top ribs. Compression in this area, either because of muscular tension or postural habits, puts pressure on these nerves and blood vessels. This may cause reduced sensation in the arms, and in some cases it can cause numbness.

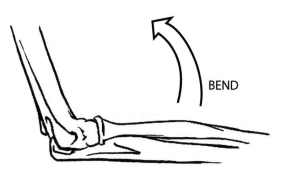

Figure 6.7. *Bending elbows*

The third arm joint is at the elbow, the point where the upper arm bone (humerus) meets the two lower arm bones (radius and ulna). Oboe players bend at the elbows in order to bring the oboe reed to the embouchure. It's important to maintain freedom at the first two arm joints, but they should exhibit little movement when bringing the oboe to a playing position. Most of the work is achieved by simply bending at the elbows.

It's fun to play "air oboe," noticing how you use your arm structure in relation to your whole body when bringing the oboe to the playing position. Start with hands in a natural position at the sides. Bring arms and hands up to a playing position and "play" without the oboe. Notice the movements at the shoulder as you bring the instrument up. There is no need to move forward with the upper torso, scapula, or neck; though, as stated earlier, they must never be fixed, either. What part of the arms really need to move, and to what degree?

Understanding pronation and supination at the elbow joint is crucial to establishing a good hand position for the oboe. I don't like the term "hand position" for the same reason I don't like the term "posture." It implies that there is one ideal way that hands are held in relation to the instrument. When we are told to find a hand position, we tend to hold, grip, or lock the arms. We know that fingers, hands, wrists, and arms need to move in order to make music with an oboe. Therefore, it is best to understand hands not in terms of finding a position, but in terms of discovering ideal relationships between the instrument, the fingers, and the four arm joints.

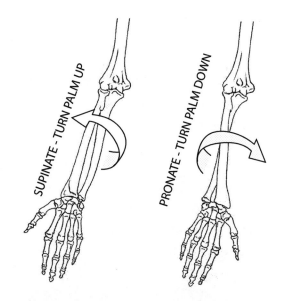

Figure 6. 8. *Pronation and supination*

When the palm of the hand is facing up, the forearm is supine. When the palm is facing down, the forearm is prone. Moving the palm from an upward position into a downward position, is called pronation. Moving the palm from a downward (prone) position to the supine position is called supination. Both pronation and supination happen at the elbow joint. Here's how.

When the palm is supine, the two bones of the forearm are parallel to each other.

These bones are called the radius and the ulna. In this palms-up position, the radius bone is on the thumb side of the forearm and the ulna bone is on the pinky side.

In order to pronate the forearm (and therefore the hand), the radius crosses over the ulna. The ulna serves as the axis for moving the hand from an upward-facing position to a prone position. The radius moves from the elbow joint, crossing over the axis of the ulna, and bringing the palm face down. One can see that a whole forearm is involved in this movement. Mapping the functions of

Understanding pronation helps us have freer fingers when playing.

pronation and supination as happening at the wrist can cause severe wrist pain and injury because of the misuse this mis-mapping imposes. Pronation is not accomplished by the hand alone, or just by the wrist, but by the whole forearm.

Figure 6.9 shows the ideal rest relationship of hand to forearm in order to pronate and supinate with complete ease. Notice the uninterrupted line from the elbow to the tip of the pinky finger. This is the way arms and hands should most often look when playing the oboe. I say "most often" because, for certain passagework, hands may have to be at a slight angle in relation to forearms. This is okay as long as the hands eventually return to the natural rest relationship shown in figure 6.9. It is when the hands are permanently fixed at an unnatural angle to the forearm that oboe players get into trouble. A fixed, unnatural position makes playing technical passagework more difficult than it needs to be, and may result in pain or injury.

"Ulnar deviation" describes a hand position in which the thumb is aligned with the forearm rather than the rest relationship described above (the pinky aligned with the forearm). Mis-mapping this relationship of hand to forearm results in chronic ulnar deviation. There are many reasons oboe players should avoid playing with chronic ulnar deviation. To begin to understand why, do the following simple experiment.

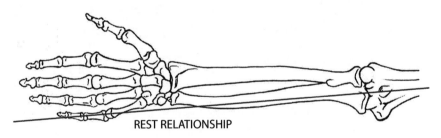

REST RELATIONSHIP

Figure 6.9. *Rest relationship*

1. Place your entire forearm and hand on a table, palm facing up.
2. Align the thumb with the elbow, as someone with chronic ulnar deviation would.
3. Pronate (move the palm to a downward facing position).
4. Do this a couple of times, noticing how it feels to make the movement.
5. Place the arm on the table again in the supine position, this time aligning the pinky naturally with the elbow.
6. Pronate the hand and forearm.
7. You will feel how much easier it is to pronate in this position—it is completely effortless.

Unfortunately, traditional oboe teaching puts a lot of emphasis on the thumbs and doesn't pay much attention to the relationship of elbows to pinky fingers. We've already discussed how the thumbs play a central role in balancing the oboe. Many optional accessories focused on the thumb are now commercially available: alternative thumb rests, neck straps, FHRED, etc. Many instructors teach that the angle of the thumbs in relation to the instrument is key to finding a good hand position. There are also teachers spending lots of time helping students develop a good technique for moving the left thumb over the octave keys.

Nothing is particularly wrong with any of these teachings. It's just that equal time must be given to the other fingers and the rest of the arm that supports those fingers. But usually very little time is spent understanding the whole hand and the whole arm. In fact, there are far too many oboists who play with chronic ulnar deviation, not realizing what a serious problem it is. I think it is our obsession with thumbs that has resulted in this unfortunate situation. Students must be provided with adequate and accurate maps of this vital area. If our teaching emphasized alignment of pinky fingers with elbows to the same degree that we emphasize thumbs, there would be no cases of oboe players playing with ulnar deviation.

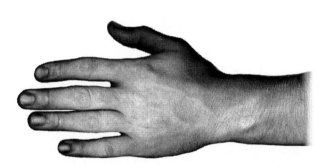

Figure 6.10. *Good hand-to-forearm alignment*

Figure 6.10 shows a hand in good alignment with the forearm. Observe the natural length in the wrist. The wrist is not being shortened due to an unnatural curve of the hand in one direction or the other. Oboe teaching based on somatics emphasizes that the hand and forearm should be brought to the keys of the instrument so that the pinky finger of the left hand can easily reach the conglomerate of keys that operate low B, low B-flat, alternate E-flat, and alternate F fingerings, *and* at the same time, maintaining alignment with the ulna bone to the elbow. The pinky of the right hand is positioned to easily reach, at all times, the conglomerate of keys that operate low C, D-flat, and E-flat fingerings while maintaining alignment with the ulna bone to the elbow.

If our teaching emphasized alignment of pinky fingers with elbows to the same degree that we emphasize thumbs, there would be no cases of oboe players playing with ulnar deviation.

Understanding pronation helps us have freer fingers when playing and also helps relieve some of the stress of reed-making. We pronate to bring the reed knife to the sharpening stone, as well as for many other movements associated with reed-making (see chapter 15, Reed-making).

Oboists move their wrists more for reed-making than for playing the instrument, but properly mapping the wrists will benefit both skills. Figure 6.11 shows that the wrist joint is the connection between the two bones of the forearm and the bones of the hand. The wrist is not the two bumps at the bottom of the forearm, as many mistakenly map them.

These bumps are part of the ulna and radius. A wrist is not a hinge joint, but a conglomerate of eight small bones (carpals) which allow for wide variations of movement: up, down, side-to-side, and circular motions.

In order to understand wrist movement, one must consider the three ways in which wrist bones interact with other bones. The three things to notice about wrists are:

1. The connection of the forearm to the wrist bones
2. The connection of the wrist bones to the rest of the hand
3. The connections between the wrist bones themselves

All of these connections should be free, allowing for fluid movements. Tension or locking at the wrist joints is particularly harmful, sometimes leading to tendonitis or carpal tunnel syndrome.

Look at the right side of the wrist bones in figure 6.11. Notice a slight gap between the ulna and the bones of the hand. This space allows for greater side-to-side movement of the hand. However, there are other things besides bones here. Nerves and connective tissue inhabit this gap. It's not a problem to occasionally press against these. But another issue created by chronic ulnar deviation is that this gap is constantly compressed.

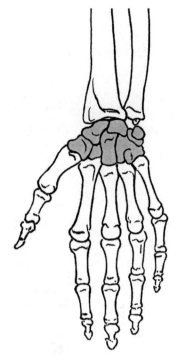

Figure 6.11. *The wrist joint*

About the Hands

Many oboe players feel that fingers do most of the work of moving keys and supporting the instrument. You should now understand that it takes much more than fingers to do the job well. Shoulder blades and collarbones locked in place, upper arms compressed against the ribs, ulnar deviation, wrists held

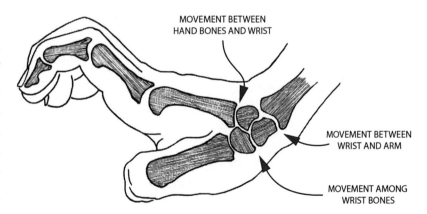

MOVEMENT BETWEEN
HAND BONES AND WRIST

MOVEMENT BETWEEN
WRIST AND ARM

MOVEMENT AMONG
WRIST BONES

Figure 6.12. *Wrist movement*

at a hinge-like angle—all these greatly inhibit free finger movement. But there is more.

There is a tremendous variety to the way fingers can move, from picking up objects to playing elegant Baroque trills. Many mistakenly think there are muscles in the hands that move the fingers. The fact is that if all the muscles needed to make these finger movements were actually in the hands, then the hands would be so bulky they could no longer accomplish the delicate movements oboe players use. The muscles which actually move the fingers are located not in the hand, but in the forearm. These forearm muscles connect to the fingers with tendons. This is another reason it is so important to avoid chronic ulnar deviation and maintain a free, relaxed wrist when playing. A hand "position" must not impinge on the fluid connection of forearm muscles to fingers. When tendons are compressed on a regular basis, they may become inflamed—a condition known as tendonitis.

A hand "position" must not impinge on the fluid connection of forearm muscles to fingers.

The term "tendonitis" is often used to describe any kind of pain found in the hands, wrists, or forearms. When one experiences pain, he should consult a medical specialist to find out precisely what it is: tendonitis, tenosynovitis, tennis elbow, or De Quervain's tenosynovitis.

There is no reason oboe playing should result in any form of tendonitis. There is nothing inherent in this act that causes the problem. Oboe players should be able to practice many hours a day, every day, without ever having tendonitis. In order to do this, we must give up the idea that fingers alone are used to play the instrument. A well-balanced body with well-aligned arms supports the fingers and allows the oboist to stay healthy.

Joints of the Thumbs and Fingers

Figure 6.13 shows that the thumb has three joints. However, if you look at your own hand, this is not as obvious. Notice the creases in the skin covering your hands, and you will see three creases in the fingers, but only two in the thumb. Moving the thumb from the second joint feels very different than movement from the third joint. Try the exercise below. You will especially notice a difference if you observe the movement from the palm side of the hand.

Figure 6.13.
The bones of the hands

1. Look at your hand, palm side up.
2. Locate the second joint of the thumb and wiggle the thumb back and forth from this joint.
3. Move from this second thumb joint to reach toward your pinky finger.
4. Can your thumb reach all the way to the pinky?
5. Can you reach the top of the pinky as well as the bottom?
6. How does this stretch feel?
7. Now locate the third joint of the thumb. You may need to palpate with your other hand in order to find it.
8. Once you've located the joint, move the thumb to the pinky finger again, this time from the third joint.

9. This movement feels significantly easier than movement from the second thumb joint. The thumb moves farther as well.

Once you map the thumb as three rather than just two joints, movement improves. The thumb's ability to support the oboe will improve as well. A thumb with three joints will feel better connected to the whole hand, the whole arm, and the whole body, resulting in a feeling of effortless support for the instrument.

While looking at your hand, shift focus from the thumb to the fingers. Look carefully at the creases on the palm side. Notice that the first and second creases correspond to the first and second joints of the fingers. They are the same on the palm side as on the backside of the hand. But the third joint is different.

Figure 6.14. *Thumb with three joints*

On the palm, there is a third crease at the point where the fingers join the hand. Turn the hand over and you clearly see the knuckles of these third joints, where the fingers move. Now notice how much lower these knuckles are than the creases seen in the palm. Mapping the hand based on how it looks from the palm side not only promotes moving the thumb from the second, rather than third joint but also promotes moving the fingers from the creases rather than the knuckles. This artificial movement is quite limiting compared to the free movement of fingers at their actual joints.

Ever have trouble reaching the E-flat key with your right pinky finger? Or maybe it's a bit of a stretch for your left pinky to reach the alternate F-key? This is often the case for players with relatively small hands who play the English horn or bass oboe. English horn players who have mis-mapped the hand from the palm side and attempt to stretch the pinky finger from the third crease of the finger will certainly feel limited, as discussed above. However, even if the third finger joint is correctly mapped, the

Mapping the hand accurately frees movement, improves coordination and also helps avoid injury.

player must accurately map where this stretch occurs for the movement to be completely free. Look at figure 6.13 again and notice how the fingers and thumb connect at the wrist. If one needs a little more space between the fingers, widen through the bones in the palm of the hand all the way to the wrist. Stretching from the finger joints at the wrist feels easier and allows one to stretch farther. This is yet another reason one should avoid any hand position that fixes the bones of the wrist or fingers.

Mapping the hand accurately frees movement, improves coordination, and also helps avoid injury. Carpal tunnel syndrome, like tendonitis, sometimes occurs due to misuse. The carpal tunnel is an area on the palm side of the hand located over the carpal bones—the eight small bones that make up the wrist. Blood vessels, tendons, and the median nerve all travel through this tunnel. Inflammation here can put pressure on these structures, compressing the nerve and causing tingling, numbness, or other symptoms.

To alleviate carpal tunnel syndrome, patients working with a doctor and physical therapist are given exercises or medications. They might be fitted with a wrist splint, or in some cases, even undergo surgery. These various remedies can relieve the symptoms of carpal tunnel syndrome. But if the root cause is an inaccurate body map that is not corrected, then the problem could very likely return.

How Do I Look?

Many oboists worry about the way their fingers look on the keys. Flattened fingers signal tension, but how *much* should the fingers be curved? Do *all* the fingers have to be curved? Some students actually increase rather than release tension by attempting to curve their fingers. They squeeze the keys and their hands begin resembling claws. Perhaps this is necessary with an instrument needing repair. But if the oboe mechanism is well adjusted, then the hand can have a very natural look.

The curve of the fingers is really quite natural. One can find it almost anytime. Just start walking around in a relaxed, comfortable manner, with hands at your sides. After a few seconds, notice your hands. You will see that the thumb and fingers are naturally curved in a perfect manner for playing an oboe. This natural curve is what you should bring to the oboe when playing.

Octave Keys

The octave key on the side of the oboe is manipulated with the left hand forefinger. The octave key on the back of the oboe is manipulated with the left hand thumb. Movement to and from these keys can be accomplished in a variety of ways.

For the back octave key, the thumb can simply slide up and down, moving from wood to octave key and back to wood. This is a simple and efficient motion. It really isn't necessary for the thumb to jump off the wood, waving with bravado in the air, before pouncing on its prey—an unsuspecting octave key! The more efficient the thumb movement, the more freely and precisely the other fingers of the left hand are able to move. As suggested earlier, this sliding from wood to octave key increases the sense of security one gets from the left hand helping to balance the instrument.

Some oboes have pointy octave keys that make this sliding movement difficult. I've taken a file to these instruments and smoothed the point away, so the player can make this move more easily. On some oboes, the octave key is placed too far away from the wood to make sliding easy, but this also can be adjusted.

One can also use a sliding movement when opening the half-hole. The left forefinger slides down just enough to open the hole and split the octave. But there are times one can use a very different motion for opening the half-hole, for pressing into the back octave key with the thumb, or for pressing the side octave key with the forefinger: forearm pronation.

Figure 6.15.
Slurring from
D to A

To play this, the tip of the left forefinger must go from opening the half-hole to closing it, while at the same time the side of the forefinger must press into the side octave key. This is all easily accomplished by taking advantage of the simple movement of a whole forearm and hand moving together, pronating slightly from the elbow. The fingers don't need to make any movement independent of the movement of pronation. They just go along for the ride as the elbow initiates a move that simultaneously brings the tip of the forefinger forward over the half-hole while bringing the side of the forefinger down toward the octave key.

Figure 6.16.
Slurring from
G to A

This can also be accomplished with a gentle pronation of the left hand. This time, the thumb starts out placed on the back octave key. As fingers, hand, wrist, and forearm pronate from the elbow, the thumb moves downward off the octave key and onto the wood. As in figure 6.15, the side of the left forefinger is brought down into the side octave key at the same time the thumb is moved.

Body Mapping Practice **2**

Fingers

The key of A-flat poses fingering challenges for oboe players. There are alternate fingerings for E-flat and F that can be used to help achieve a better legato, or to facilitate quicker movement between notes. The player must first decide which fingerings are most appropriate for a particular passage and then get comfortable using the fingering choices in a musical way.

Play figure 6.17, focusing on how your fingers relate to the keys of the instrument and are supported by good overall body balance.

Figure 6.17.
Before playing:

1. Take time to notice your balance in relation to the chair (if sitting) or the floor (if standing).
2. Repeat Alexander's orders (see chapter 4).
3. Bring the instrument to the playing position. Note that this simple action often gets oboe players into trouble before the first note of music is sounded, so really pay attention to how you manage it.

If you are balanced before bringing the instrument to the playing position, then most of the work is achieved by moving at the elbows. The upper arm structure will move very little or not at all (remember that the point where collarbone, shoulder blade, and upper arm meet should be at center, not slumped forward or pulled back). When the neck muscles are freed they do not need to move in response to the upward movement of the instrument. With the skull dynamically poised over the vertebrae of the spine, neck muscles remain free, and you feel weight—your weight and the weight of the instrument—delivered to the chair or floor.

As you play figure 6.17:

1. Continue to notice your balance
   a. Free the neck muscles
   b. Release the head forward and up
   c. Lengthen and widen through the back and legs
   d. Sense weight as delivered through the rockers at the bottom of your pelvis to the chair or through the central arches of your feet to the floor
2. Play every note with the most beautiful resonance you can find and perfect intonation (many oboes have notoriously unstable intonation on the F, G, and A-flat at the top of the staff)
3. Listen to what happens between notes
4. The timbre of all notes should match as evenly as possible, creating a seamless legato
5. Play this warm-up at least four times
6. After each playing, analyze how your mind and body are interacting to create beautiful music
7. Answer the following questions to help improve your overall awareness:
   a. Do you clearly perceive the organization of your arm from the tip of the pinky finger to the tip of the shoulder blade as you play?
   b. Are your wrists able to move freely at all times?
   c. Does the point of contact between your right thumb and the thumb rest allow all the right-hand fingers to curve naturally above the keys of the instrument?
   d. Can your pinky finger easily reach both the D-flat and E-flat keys?
   e. Does the left thumb stray unnecessarily away from the instrument?
   f. How does the left thumb respond to movements of the first finger when uncovering the half-hole?
   g. How easily does the left thumb move from the wood of the instrument to the octave key?
   h. What is the quality of your hand movements?
   i. How far away from the keys do your fingers move?
   j. Could they move less far away?
   k. On a scale of one to ten, how relaxed do your hands feel? (experiment by playing the excerpt with higher levels of tension and relaxation)
   l. If you are right-handed:
      1. Play the excerpt again, this time noticing precisely how you use the left hand
      2. When does it move?
      3. How does it move?
   m. If you are left-handed, notice precisely how you use the right hand

Now you'll want to take the ease you've gained from practicing this warm-up and put it into a more musical situation. Most people are familiar with the beautiful melody in figure 6.18. We remember Judy Garland's effortless performance in *The Wizard of Oz*. When set in the key of A-flat, it is not easy to sound as beautiful and effortless on the oboe, but this should be the player's goal. This goal is achieved by setting the right conditions: free finger and hand movements, supported by good balance.

Figure 6.18.

Chapter 7

Thumb Rests, Neck Straps, and FHRED—Oh, My!

Over the past several years many alternatives to the traditional thumb rest have been developed: neck straps, Dutch thumb rests, adjustable thumb rests, FHRED, and other forms of support. Trying them all takes a lot of patience and money, both of which tend to be in short supply among oboe players! So I will attempt to guide you through the ever-thickening forest of possibilities.

There is one thing that we can glean from the fact that so many options to the thumb rest have been developed. The traditional thumb rest is not working for many, many oboe players. It is very common for oboe players to develop unsightly, sometimes painful calluses on the right thumb due to pressure against the thumb rest. Depending on the size of the player's hand, it can be awkward to find a comfortable position for the thumb that still allows the hand to be in a natural position. Over time, compromised hand positions can lead to pain in the thumb, hand, wrist, or forearm. This may be due to strained or torn ligaments or may become full-blown tendonitis, carpal tunnel syndrome, or tennis elbow.

Adjustable and Dutch Thumb Rest

The adjustable thumb rest and the Dutch thumb rest are two variations on the traditional thumb rest that have been helpful for oboe players. Some are mostly comfortable with the thumb rest but need it placed slightly lower. Thus the adjustable thumb rest was developed. It is positioned in the same place as the thumb rest that comes with the instrument and uses the same screw holes, but the pad is designed to adjust up and down so the player can find a more comfortable spot for the right hand in relation to the keys. You may find a position that seems quite comfortable for months, even years, but then the hand begins feeling cramped. So you merely readjust the pad up or down slightly, and this often frees up the hand again.

Figure 7.1.
Dutch thumb rest

Thumb rest images courtesy of Forrests Music.

Some want the hand higher up, so they will have two holes drilled higher up on the bottom joint and position the adjustable thumb rest there.

The Dutch thumb rest also fits in the same spot as the traditional thumb rest but has a greatly extended pad for the thumb as well as a flat body plate which adds additional thickness to the grip on the oboe. For many this is just what they need to pivot the thumb slightly forward or back, bringing the whole hand into a position that's more comfortable for making contact with the keys.

FHRED, MUTS, and Other Supports

An alternative to thumb rests is provided by a variety of support systems designed to shift the weight of the instrument from the thumb rest to a peg. Some of these supports attach directly to the thumb rest, others to the bell. The peg may sit on the chair, on the floor, or rest in a pouch at the waist.

FHRED is the most popular of these systems. Its name is an acronym for Finger and Hand Retraining Ergonomic Device. Many double reed players are thankful for FHRED, feeling that it has added years to their playing careers. This ingenious device is easy to attach to the instrument and is quite sturdy. Since the weight of the instrument is transferred to the chair, the hands feel quite free.

FHRED is designed for sitting. If you want to stand, you can purchase SAMI (Standup Accessory for Musical Instruments). A note for ladies, or anyone else wearing a dress when performing: FHRED can be used with a dress as long as the dress has a gathered skirt and the skirt is not made with a slippery fabric such as taffeta. To use a FHRED with a straight skirt or a slippery fabric, a SAMI is recommended.

The one complaint commonly leveled against FHRED is that it limits the amount of movement one can make, since the peg must at all times stay in contact with the chair. This is a particular problem when playing chamber music. When FHRED is attached, it is not possible to use the instrument for cueing fellow players.

Figure 7.2.
FHRED

MUTS (Michael's Ultimate Thumb Saver) is a privately made support which allows for more movement, but it cannot be used when standing.

Bell support pegs are a lifesaver when playing the bass oboe, and are becoming popular with some English horn players as well. These feature a ring that tightens over the bell of the instrument. Attached to the ring is a peg that rests on the floor. Like FHRED, the weight of the instrument is transferred away from the hands, in this case, released directly to the floor. The thumb rest on most bass oboes is quite a bit higher than the keys, forcing the hand into a position of ulnar deviation (to understand why one should avoid ulnar deviation, see chapter 6). Using a bell support peg allows one to put the right hand into a comfortable position in relation to the keys, the thumb freely placed on the wood instead of placing it next to the provided thumb rest.

Those who find the weight of an English horn cumbersome over time often find relief using either the FHRED or the bell support peg.

Figure 7.3.
Bell support peg

The Weight Reduction Instrumental System Technology, or WRIST, has recently been developed by the Chicago Reed Company. It is a sturdy and ingenious design that attaches to a music stand, and is widely adjustable. The bell of an oboe or English horn gently rests against it, diverting the instrument's weight away from the hands. The WRIST seems especially useful for English horn players, as it provides more mobility than either FHRED or a bell support peg.

> **You should never feel that the reed is being fixed in one position because the strap is not long enough to allow for some play at the embouchure.**

Neck Straps

Many English horn players use neck straps to help support the weight of the instrument. Be aware that although all English horns are heavier than oboes, not all English horns weigh the same. Some are significantly heavier than others, depending on the manufacturer and type of wood used.

English horn players are not the only ones to use neck straps. Oboists and oboe d'amore players sometimes use them as well.

There are many types of neck straps available. Be certain to use a neck strap that has a strap long enough to reach the horn. You should never feel that the reed is being fixed in one position because the strap is not long enough to allow for some play at the embouchure. Stretchy, bungee-style straps are usually preferred.

The most commonly used neck straps rest against the neck muscles. Others types include the yoke style, which rests over the collarbones and the back, and the harness style, which utilizes the whole torso for support.

Straps that rest against the back of the neck tend to have a negative effect on posture. The little tug persistently felt against the neck muscles when wearing one of these straps seems to subconsciously pull the head downward. When wearing this neck strap you will need to make an extra effort to constantly be on guard for tension in the neck muscles so that you can find good balance over the chair or floor.

The yoke-style neck strap makes more sense ergonomically, as it shifts the weight away from the neck to the collarbones. These sturdy bones easily accept the weight, just as with violins and violas. However, these straps are difficult to find and may need to be custom made, as it is not possible to have one size that fits all body types.

The harness strap is probably the most comfortable one of all, but many double reed players avoid it because

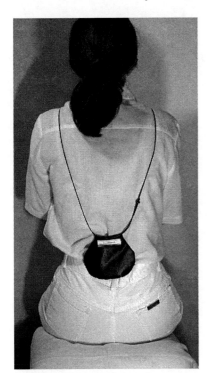

Figure 7.4. *Counterbalance*
Photo courtesy of Oboe Counterbalance.

it is cumbersome and doesn't look good with formal clothes.

The counterbalance brand may be the best of available neck straps. It consists of a pouch hanging at the lower back attached to the thumb rest by a lightweight cord. The pouch is filled with lead pellets, measured to offset the weight of the instrument. The counterbalance strap is compact, easy to attach, and can be used sitting or standing.

Kooiman—a new model for thumb rests

The branches of a tree are thickest and strongest where they join the trunk of the tree. If I'm climbing a tree, I stand confidently on this part of the branch. I wouldn't walk out toward the very edge of the branch, for I know it would break under my weight.

Your thumb is constructed in a similar manner. The part closest to your hand can bear weight much more easily than the tip of the thumb. Yet traditional thumb rests deliver all the weight of the instrument to the tip of the thumb. Recognizing the fallacy of this, a Dutch manufacturer, Ton Kooiman, has developed a new mechanism that transfers the instrument's weight to the part of the thumb that can best bear the load.

Of all the products described in this chapter, I feel that Ton Kooiman's products (the Etude thumb rest, oboe thumb rest, and English horn thumb rest) are the most elegant, practical and universal. They can be used whether you're sitting or standing, playing chamber, solo, or orchestral music, and it doesn't matter what you're wearing! Most importantly, they completely relieve any tension created by traditional thumb rests. These devices actually help you find the best possible position for moving your fingers on the instrument—no calluses, no pain, no injury.

Figure 7.5. Kooiman oboe thumb rest

Kooiman thumb rests are supported by an excellent website describing the various products and providing many suggestions for how to properly attach and adjust them. The website claims "...the oboe thumb rest can be adjusted in all possible directions to meet the highest individual demands." This is true and is one of the great advantages of this thumb rest over the less expensive Etude version. It can also be a source of frustration at first. Because the thumb rest is made to adjust in so many different directions, it takes great patience to find the best position to suit your hand and your method of playing. It is useful to have a friend or teacher help you make these adjustments.

Figure 7.6. Kooiman Etude thumb rest

Since this thumb rest is relatively expensive, I often recommend that players try the much cheaper Etude thumb rest first. It is also quite comfortable, but doesn't adjust in as many ways as the oboe or English horn thumb rests. It is also less sturdy. Even though it is made with a rather strong plastic, I have heard complaints that the plastic sometimes breaks. If this happens during a performance it can be a big problem. For that reason, I suggest buying two, so you have one that can serve as a backup if the other breaks. A corner broke off one that I was using. I put it back together with superglue and it's held up fine ever since. If it broke during a performance of a Beethoven symphony, however, it would be pretty impractical to superglue it back together while counting rests!

If one likes the Etude model and plays oboe or English horn on a regular basis, I strongly recommend upgrading to the sturdier and more versatile professional models. Be forewarned that in order to anchor these thumb rests a third screw hole must be drilled into the instrument. This is an easy task for a professional repairperson and does no damage to the instrument, nor will it affect the tone in any way. However, some repair technicians may give you a hard time about it.

Here's an e-mail I received recently from a student concerning this:

Dr. Caplan:

Well, I brought my oboe to "X" today to have him drill an extra hole in the back and attach the Kooiman thumb rest. I'm glad you prepared me for him—his initial reaction was to rant and rave about how we oboists with our "wacky" thumb rests devalue our instruments by drilling more holes in the back of the instrument. However, his rant didn't deter me from wanting the thumb rest. What good is a higher resale value to me if I can't play the oboe without pain and damage to my wrist and hand? (I don't think this occurs to him.) Besides which, the hole he drills could be filled with epoxy, just like they've done for all the pins they've had to put in my oboe already.

So I told him I'd really like him to do the work, but if he wouldn't I'd go to someone else. Then he disappeared into the back by his desk and put the thumb rest on my oboe. When he re-emerged he was very nice and polite. That man gives "mood swing" new meaning!

—Sincerely, Maria

Chapter 8

Case Study Number 2: Alex's Arms

Alex had tendonitis. He explained where it affected him (his forearm), and how he had tried to treat it. He saw a doctor and a physical therapist who confirmed the tendonitis and suggested he take Advil for the pain. The physical therapist suggested that developing more upper arm strength might relieve some of the strain. So this therapist had him lifting weights and swimming. Both experts recommended that he limit the amount of playing he does or else stop altogether until the pain disappears.

This is all good advice. Advil will help relieve short-term pain. If tendonitis has developed to the degree that it is consistently painful to play, then one should stop playing altogether for a short period. The physical therapist's work certainly can't hurt either. Although I don't think muscular strength is necessary to play the oboe, perhaps the weightlifting and swimming could encourage Alex to use his whole arm to support the weight of the instrument rather than with the thumb alone—a tendency among many players.

As Alex described these things to me I noticed that he was a very serious person. He worked hard at oboe playing and had been very successful for his age level, having won several competitions. He presently studies at a major conservatory. I observed him play. What I saw right away was a very awkward-looking right hand position. The hand was cocked up high with fingers straight. As I walked around him to observe the hand from a different angle, I noticed his thumb looked odd. Alex used a Dutch thumb rest, but instead of his thumb being curved in a natural position or even held straight, it was overextended in a backwards curve. This thumb position made it almost impossible for Alex to hold his right hand in a better way.

"It seems your thumb is double-jointed. Are all your fingers double-jointed?" I asked.

Alex answered, "Yes."

"Is it possible for you to curve your thumb in a more natural way?"

He showed me that it was possible.

"Now would you maintain that curved thumb to hold the oboe?" I requested.

He tried and his thumb immediately went to its habitual double-jointed extension.

"Okay, let's try again. Show me away from the oboe that your thumb will curve naturally." He did. "Now let's take that to the thumb rest and maintain an awareness of the thumb as you play the oboe." He did.

"How does your thumb feel?" I inquired.

He said, "It feels really uncomfortable."

"Does it feel painful?"

"No, not at all."

"Then uncomfortable is okay."

It was uncomfortable because it was so foreign for him to hold the instrument in this way. I suggested that he practice only little bits at a time, but always with the intention of keeping a natural curve in the thumb. I assured him that if he did this with patience and consistency that the uncomfortable feeling would eventually go away. He told me one of his former teachers had also suggested that he correct his thumb in this manner, but when he told them it wasn't comfortable, the teacher wasn't insistent about it. I told him I would be insistent about it. This change might be slow at first, but it would be worth it. Advil may provide some short-term relief, but changing a habit such as this will have long-term results.

But this was not enough. As we continued to work, I noticed that Alex had ulnar deviation in both hands, and this was manifest not only in his hand position when he played the oboe, but in many other activities as well (picking up his case, etc.). We had a Body Mapping lesson on the arm and ulnar deviation. It made sense to him. I suggested that he try a Kooiman thumb rest, which he did. Because this type of thumb rest transfers the weight of the oboe from the tip to the second joint of the thumb, Alex found it much more comfortable to maintain the natural curve and avoid his old habit of overextension. His whole hand position appeared to improve significantly, and he was experiencing less pain from tendonitis.

I left him to go off to another year at the conservatory feeling we had made some real progress.

When I saw him again a few months later, he explained that his teachers at the Conservatory had insisted that he play in several ensembles and that the tendonitis had flared up again. I was angry that the school had insisted he play when they knew of his tendonitis problem. I also wasn't sure how much Alex really protested. He was a dutiful student who did what his teachers told him to do, and I think he was flattered that he was being asked to play with some of the school's better ensembles.

I watched him play again, looking for some sign that he was reverting back to his old habit. However, his hand movements actually looked improved. He then mentioned to me that he had stopped making reeds recently because his forearm seemed to especially hurt when he made lots of reeds. So I asked if I could watch him make a reed. He said his knife was dull. So I asked if I could watch him sharpen the knife. This is where I saw two disturbing things.

When he held the knife, his hand went into a position with severe ulnar deviation. I also saw that he had a dull knife but was using a relatively fine stone to sharpen it. I mentioned that if I had a knife that dull, I would first use a rougher stone for sharpening and then use the fine stone. It saves time, and is probably more effective at producing a sharp edge.

He answered, "I know it would save time, but I don't mind taking more time to sharpen the knife." There are problems with this related to the technique of knife sharpening, but what I want to focus on is the fact that Alex was making many more strokes than necessary to sharpen the knife—all using a fixed hand position that was aggravating his tendonitis!

We worked on finding a way to hold the knife that conformed to a well-aligned hand and forearm. It meant changing the position of the stone slightly, but Alex was able to make these adjustments easily. It would prove to make a world of difference in the health of his arms. Alex no longer has tendonitis, nor any other pain in his arms. He's making better reeds now, as well.

Agenda Helper 3

Fingers

Mark the statements that are true for you. Work on the ones that aren't checked.

- ❑ My body map contains a whole arm: collar bone, shoulder blade, humerus, radius, ulna, wrist, and hand.
- ❑ I know that I play and gesture with four arm joints, not three.
- ❑ My arms feel light as I play and make reeds.
- ❑ My arms feel supported as I play and make reeds.
- ❑ My body feels articulated as I play and make reeds.
- ❑ I clearly perceive the organization of my arm from the tip of my little finger to the tip of my shoulder blade.
- ❑ My arms display a natural organization, as in childhood.
- ❑ I always perceive my arms as a part of the whole of me.
- ❑ I perceive the weight of the oboe supported by the whole of me, not just my thumb.
- ❑ I move well at the joints of my upper arms and shoulder blades.
- ❑ I perceive clearly the movement of my upper arms and shoulder blades.
- ❑ I am free of pain in my elbow as I play.
- ❑ I am free of pain in my upper body as I play.
- ❑ I am free of strain in my elbow as I play.
- ❑ I can pronate and supinate fully at my elbow without strain.
- ❑ My lower arm muscles are relaxed when they are not working.
- ❑ My wrists are long and free as I move.
- ❑ I do not over-stabilize my wrists as I play and make reeds.
- ❑ I use all three joints of my wrists as I play and make reeds.
- ❑ My hands and forearms are at a neutral position when I have no need to bend at the wrists.
- ❑ My arms do not feel heavy as I play.
- ❑ My hands never hurt as I play.
- ❑ My hands never tire as I play.
- ❑ I am tactilely awake in my fingers as I play.
- ❑ I am kinesthetically awake in my fingers as I play.
- ❑ I use appropriate effort in my hands as I play.
- ❑ I use appropriate effort in my hands as I make reeds.
- ❑ My upper arm bones rotate in their sockets appropriately as I play.
- ❑ I am free of strain in my upper body as I play.

Chapter 9

Embouchure

I am in favor of a mobile, flexible embouchure which will give you the possibility to scale tone color as on the violin.

Marcel Tabuteau[7]

Entering the concert hall early, I heard the random chirping, scraping, and buzzing sounds of my colleagues warming up. A horn player repeatedly played a short excerpt from the symphony scheduled for that day's rehearsal. He kept messing up an octave leap at the end of the phrase. Just as I was passing him to get to my chair, I heard him play the excerpt once more, making the same mistake. But then he said in an angry tone, "more air, less face!" He played the excerpt again, and it was perfect.

"More air, less face!" This phrase which helped my horn-playing friend is a reminder that often what we perceive as embouchure problems are actually problems with air. In fact, air is an integral part of any embouchure.

The word embouchure is from a French root meaning "mouth of a river." Just as the mouth of a river is the point where a river becomes an ocean, an embouchure is the point where air becomes vibration. This chapter explores how vibration is created through the interaction of air with face.

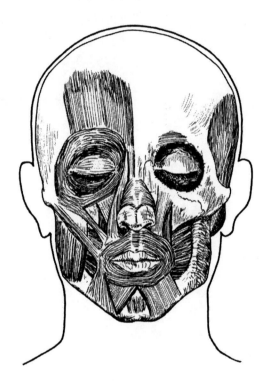

"More air, less face!"

Reed My Lips

Chapter 6 discussed how the hands touch and support the oboe, but the embouchure is the only place where the oboe and the body are truly joined. This oboe joint is the spot where the two blades of the reed meet the two lips. Joints are usually named after the entities that are joined—atlanto-occipital (atlas and occiput), or sterno-clavicular (sternum and clavicle).

This reminds me of married couples who hyphenate their names, or when political pundits refer to Bill and Hillary Clinton as "Billary." Since the place where an oboe player joins with an oboe involves reed and lips, I'll name it the "reed my lips joint."

Some oboe players are very concerned that the "reed my lips joint" has a particular look. I've seen teaching studios with pictures on the wall of a "perfect" embouchure as an example for students. Although there are things about the look of an embouchure that can signal poor use or excessive tension, there is not one ideal look for an embouchure. Embouchures are highly individual, since they are composed of varied and personalized jaw lines, lip sizes, and dental structures. Moreover, embouchures should be somewhat flexible, able to adjust to musical needs. This "reed my lips joint" may look slightly different when playing in the upper rather than the low register, or may adjust in some subtle way when making a diminuendo or creating a change of tone color.

These adjustments are actually movements, movements made by more than lips. They are made by muscles in the face, movements of the jaw, and movements within the oral cavity behind the lips.

There are many theories about the proper formation of an oboe embouchure. Some embouchures are like a smile; others, like a snarl. Some oboe players take a lot of reed into the mouth, others take in as little as possible. Some anchor the reed toward the bottom lip, others to the top lip. Some embouchures are based on using highly resistant reeds, others use very free blowing, flexible reeds. These are just a few of the numerous differences between oboe embouchures. However, the anatomy of the face is the same for everyone. No matter what playing technique you prefer, your embouchure will be enhanced with a better understanding of this anatomy.

Muscles of the Face

One clearly sees in figure 9.1 that there are many muscles in the face. They appear to be interrelated, and most are. Many of these muscles can and should be recruited when playing the oboe or English horn.

It's a mistake to think that only the "lipstick lips" form an embouchure. Lips are more than the band of pink skin around the mouth. They are controlled by the thick muscle encircling the mouth, called the *orbicularis oris*. The tremendous variety of movements we make with our lips and cheeks are controlled by several muscles above, below, and to the sides of the orbicularis oris.

People who have mis-mapped the embouchure to only the lipstick lips do not take advantage of a full range of embouchure movements. They tend to tire easily and have trouble controlling intonation,

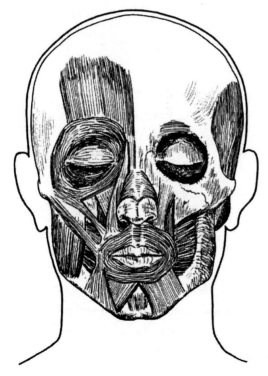

Figure 9.1. Muscles of the face

64

dynamics, and tone color. If you've always thought of an embouchure as just being the lipstick lips, then try this little experiment.

1. Play a note on the oboe, making a crescendo and then a diminuendo, consciously trying to use only the lips as an embouchure.
2. Now play again, this time allowing all the muscles of the face to help make the crescendo and diminuendo.
3. Don't try to force these other muscles to do anything in particular. Merely think of a beautiful sound with a steady crescendo and diminuendo, and invite these other muscles to participate in the process.

Simply suggesting to the other muscles that they can be a part of your music making is enough to recruit them. Most people find greater ease, greater control, and better endurance when the whole face is engaged in forming the embouchure.

Myth Buster

The lips form the embouchure.

Myth Replacement

Many facial muscles are recruited when forming an embouchure.

When people map the lipstick lips as the basis of an embouchure, they have trouble gauging the amount of reed that goes in the mouth. This is a touchy subject because of the many variables involved, including one's conception of tone as well as the type of reed used. However, I bring it up because it is important to realize that one must not base the decision of how much reed should go in the mouth on the look of the lipstick lips. I've heard oboists say that thin lips are better for playing the oboe, or thick lips are better, or that one shouldn't see any lip when the embouchure is formed. The fact is that many different sorts of lips can play the oboe beautifully if the person behind those lips has a good conception of sound in the brain and understands how the whole face helps form the embouchure.

For those who have only thought of lips forming an embouchure, it is important to understand the interrelationship of all the face muscles. However, it's equally important to recognize that these muscles can act independently of each other as well. Wind players can actively engage muscles of the lower face without affecting the muscles in the upper part of the face. Oboe players can have the flexible embouchure needed to play the many leaps in the Mozart *Oboe Quartet* and still have relaxed and expressive eyes and faces. One does not have to furrow the brow or excessively raise the eyebrows in order to have a beautiful tone on the English horn.

The facial muscles at the "reed my lips" joint are mobile, not fixed. So too is the area behind the mouth, described as the oral cavity. The oral cavity has walls (cheeks), a floor (tongue), and ceiling (hard and soft palates), but these structures are not stable like the walls, floor, and ceiling of a practice room. The oral cavity is quite mobile and must be able to move freely in order to respond to the demands of the music. Double reed players use this space to enhance tone and create colors by changing the position of the tongue or raising the soft palate, often mimicking the shape of different vowel sounds. These subtle movements of the oral cavity can also affect the formation of the embouchure.

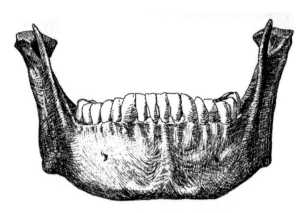

Figure 9.2. There is only one jaw

The Jaw

The jaw is an integral part of the embouchure. The first thing to notice about figure 9.2 is that there is only one jaw. The lower teeth are attached to this jaw. The upper teeth are attached to the skull, not to an "upper jaw." Some people map themselves as having "jaws," and consequently move the embouchure in an ineffective and sometimes injurious manner. In order to move their imagined upper jaw, they may throw their skull off balance at the A-O joint, which, as we saw in chapter 3, can have a negative effect on the whole body. You only have one jaw.

The next thing to notice is how the jaw attaches to the skull. The jaw is also called the *mandible*. At the top of the far right side of figure 9.3 is the point of contact between the mandible and the part of the skull called the temporal bone. This joint, therefore, is known as the temporomandibular joint, commonly called the TMJ. Figure 9.3 shows the left side of a jaw, but the right side has the same structure. So you have a temporomandibular joint on each side of your face. You can locate it easily by placing a finger in front of and slightly above your ear lobe. Open and close your mouth, until you feel the mandible bone moving away from the temporal bone.

Some people move the jaw in an inefficient manner because they have not mapped this location properly (see figure 9.4). If you map the TMJ at the base of the ear or the middle of the cheek you will try to move the jaw from these points, creating unnecessary tension and inhibiting the flexibility of the embouchure.

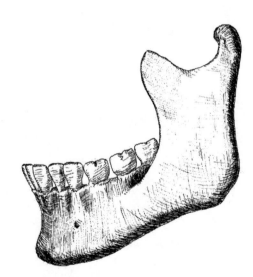

Figure 9.3. A side view of the jaw

Oboe players should understand that the jaw is capable of several movements, most of which are not needed for oboe playing. The jaw can move forward, side to side, and quite far down. But the only jaw movement needed for oboe playing is a natural dropping down from the temporomandibular joints. The jaw does not need to move forward first and then drop down.

The jaw simply drops down because gravity takes it there. This movement should feel quite effortless. The *masseter* muscle is located in the cheekbone and is responsible for lifting the jaw to clamp the mouth shut. When this muscle

There is only one jaw.

relaxes, the jaw effortlessly falls to the natural position we use to form an embouchure.

Problems with the jaw sometimes get quite serious, and are described as temporomandibular joint dysfunction, often erroneously called TMJ. Remember that the temporomandibular joint is a joining of the jaw with the skull. Sometimes discomfort and dysfunction in these joints result from injury that need to be surgically repaired, but often stems from misuse of the joints based on mis-mapping or tension imposed from tense neck muscles and imbalance at the A-O joint. TMJ dysfunction due to misuse can only be relieved when the skull is free and actively poised over a balanced spine. Once again, the importance of free neck muscles cannot be overemphasized. A free neck is essential in order to release tension at the TMJ.

The condition of your teeth also has an impact on oboe embouchure. The size of teeth affects how much the lips can be rolled in to form the embouchure. An over- or under-bite affects the angle of the reed in relation to the embouchure. Crooked or overly pointed teeth can sometimes be painful for the oboe player, so a dentist should be consulted on how to correct these issues. All oboists should follow their dentist's advice for maintaining healthy teeth, including brushing and

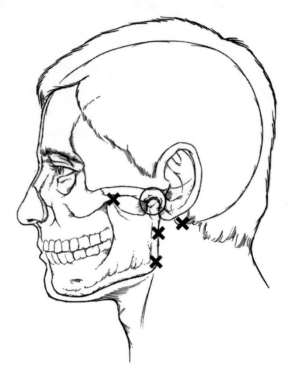

Figure 9.4. *Mapping the TMJ (bold x's indicate places mistakenly mapped as the TMJ)*

flossing regularly. I know many oboists who carry a toothbrush and/or dental floss in their gig bag.

Some oboists consider the teeth as the foundation for the embouchure rather than the lips. What is the foundation for your embouchure? Does the embouchure even need a foundation? Some feel the need to anchor the reed slightly toward the lower lip, others toward the upper lip. If one thinks of the lips as a foundation for the embouchure, there is a danger that they will be held more rigidly than necessary in order to create a firm structural support. This is particularly true if there is the misperception that the lips alone create an embouchure without including the other muscles of the face. The teeth, attached to the bony structures of the jaw and the skull, have the advantage of already being a solid and reliable foundation, thus allowing the lips to freely respond to musical demands.

Reed My Lips

This "reed my lips" joint, known as an embouchure, controls everything we do as oboe players. This is where air, tongue, and face meet a reed to produce vibration, the core of our music making. By closely monitoring what goes on at this joint we can determine the appropriate resistance a reed must have in order to make a beautiful sound—thus we improve our reed-making. By always monitoring what happens at this joint we figure out exactly how much air pressure is needed to create a great sound in all registers of the instrument—thus we improve our breathing. By constantly monitoring the movements of the tongue at this joint, we develop a sensitivity to how the reed is affected by the tongue's actions—thus we improve articulation. When we monitor the movement of face muscles, we improve our control of dynamics, intonation, resonance, and phrasing.

There's a good reason that many great oboe teachers have their students experiment with playing the reed without an instrument attached to it—the same reason brass players sometimes practice on the mouthpiece only. *Oboemotions* encourages a whole-body awareness while playing music. But your understanding and awareness of the whole body must be in the service of producing healthy vibrations from the reed at the embouchure.

> **When we monitor the movement of face muscles, we improve our control of dynamics, intonation, resonance, and phrasings.**

Some players get distracted from the "reed my lips joint," thinking the tone is primarily controlled by actions in the stomach or throat. They put a lot of energy into "pushing from the diaphragm," or "opening the throat," forgetting to even notice the vibration of the reed and how the actions of tongue, lips, and air are affecting that vibration. Chapter 10 sorts out how the throat and abdomen relate to the movements of breathing. Since air is a part of the embouchure, a better understanding of the breathing structures improves one's understanding of embouchure as well.

Body Mapping Practice 3

Embouchure

Now add crescendo and diminuendo to the same warm-up introduced earlier (shown in figure 9.5). Use this simple exercise to gain a better understanding of how embouchure and air pressure interact to create a great sound at all dynamic levels and in all registers.

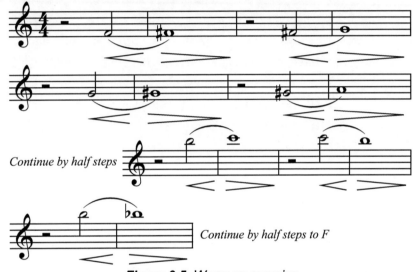

Figure 9.5. *Warm-up exercise*

A basic air pressure must be maintained so the sound is always steady and resonant. How much do you need to recruit the embouchure muscles in order to create dynamic shadings? Is your embouchure confined only to the lipstick lips, or are you taking advantage of the many face muscles that can contribute to embouchure movements?

Figure 9.6 gives the famous oboe solo from Franz Schubert's *Unfinished Symphony* (*Symphony No. 8 in B Minor*), and is a beautiful study in control and the expressive use of dynamics. Practice it and notice the subtle ways your embouchure can help control intonation, dynamics, and tone color.

Figure 9.6. *Oboe solo from Schubert's* Symphony No. 8 in B minor

Agenda Helper 4

Embouchure

Mark the statements that are true for you. Work on the ones that aren't checked.

- ❑ I have only one jaw in my body map.
- ❑ I have accurately mapped the location of the joints where my jaw and skull meet.
- ❑ I open my jaw with ease.
- ❑ I actively monitor the "reed my lips joint" as I play to control the interaction of air, tongue, and embouchure with the vibrating reed in order to play great music.
- ❑ My map of an embouchure involves many muscles of my face, not just lipstick lips.
- ❑ My embouchure moves freely whenever necessary.
- ❑ I close my jaw with ease.

Chapter 10

Air

This art of respiration once acquired, the student has gone a considerable step on the road to Parnassus.

Enrico Caruso[8]

Prologue: The Life Force

Inhalation. Exhalation.

Respiration—the perpetual cycle of inhaling and exhaling—keeps us alive. It keeps our music alive as well. In essence, the oboe's song is merely sustained exhalation.

Because breath is so crucial to oboe playing, everything is affected when it is impaired. Poor tone quality, faulty intonation, clumsy finger movement, and sluggish articulation—each improves when breath control improves.

Many teachers develop theories and use metaphors to describe how we bring air into the body and then turn it into music. A partial list of these follows. None make much sense, and some are completely wrongheaded:

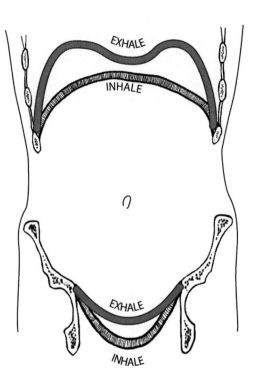

- Breathe into the lowest part of the lung first, then the middle, then the upper part
- Imagine a column of air from the bottom of your torso to the instrument
- Focus air at the front of the throat
- Open the throat
- Push from the diaphragm
- Breathe from the belly
- Feel like you are bringing air in below the navel
- Blow air to the bell of the instrument
- Raise the sternum in order to get a good breath
- Always keep the ribs open

With Body Mapping you can understand the structures of breathing and map its movements. Then there is no need for theories or metaphors; you simply work with reality.

It's true that playing the oboe feels different from playing any other instrument. The reed requires such a small amount of air to vibrate in comparison to that of other instruments. We feel like we're holding our breath all the time. As the legendary oboist Marcel Tabuteau said, "oboe players are always suffocating with the surplus of air." Because of this, oboe players must manage air in unique ways. But this does not mean that the mechanics of breathing are in any way different for oboe players. The better we understand the mechanics of breathing, the better we work with the body's natural breathing process, the more successfully we can manage the breath to accommodate great oboe playing.

> **Because breath is so crucial to oboe playing, everything is affected when it is impaired.**

This chapter tells the story of this life force: its swift, complicated journey into our body, and then its delayed escape. It also explains how our body supports the journey and is nurtured by it. This story of inspiration ends, Syrinx-like, with vibrating reeds and sound waves singing more stories—treasured stories of Bach or Mozart, or newly improvised tales for future generations.

From the Top: Nose, Mouth, and Throat

Whether inhaling or exhaling, air moves through the body from top to bottom. The movements of breathing happen almost all at once, but are wavelike and sequential, also from top to bottom.

Wind, coming in through either the nose or mouth, fills the pharyngeal space. The pharynx has three sections:

1. *Naso:* the upper part, behind the nose
2. *Oral:* the middle part, behind the mouth
3. *Laryngeal:* the lowest section, behind the larynx and above the esophagus

The middle and lower areas are commonly called the throat. Air fills these spaces on its journeys of inhalation and exhalation. The pharyngeal space is lined with sense receptors giving us information. We notice if air is coming in or going out, how much there is, how fast or slow it moves, whether it is warm or cold.

Air makes its way to the trachea which leads to the lungs. The trachea is also called the windpipe. It is less than five inches long in an adult, and you can use your fingers to gently feel its cartilaginous surface just below the Adam's apple at the front of your neck. The Adam's apple is part of the larynx, the voice box that rests on top of the trachea. This is the only passageway wind can use to travel to the lungs. Whether you take a big or small breath, all air takes the same journey.

Figure 10.1 shows what an open throat really looks like. In the laryngeal pharynx, you see the trachea in front with the esophagus behind it. Close behind this is the spine. Above the laryngeal pharynx, also sitting in front of the spine, is the oral pharynx, lined with swallowing muscles.

Food consumption is one of this area's most important duties. The tongue, soft palate, and the muscles lining the back and sides of the throat transport food and liquids on their journey through the body to the stomach. Food must find its way to the esophagus. Located at the top of the larynx is the epiglottis, a flap of tissue that closes during swallowing. This prevents choking by keeping food out of the windpipe.

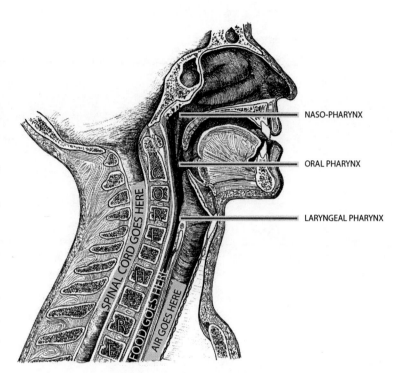

Figure 10.1. Pharynx labeled

Since the esophagus and windpipe are so close together, one must be clear about their structure and function. The trachea is in front, with the esophagus behind. The trachea is for air, the esophagus for food. People who mis-map these may suffer serious breathing problems.

Another breathing problem can occur because of a different mis-mapping in this area. As mentioned earlier, the function of muscles that line the back and sides of the throat is to assist with swallowing. However, some have mapped their function as helping to move air. Those with this mis-mapping are literally "swallowing" air, tightening these muscles on inhalation. The result is noisy breathing that is unmusical, and a tense throat that interferes with good tone production. The throat must be re-mapped with regard to function in order to eliminate interference of throat tension while breathing.

One thing you won't see in figure 10.1 is a "column of air." This metaphor is another source for tension in the throat when we try to create a column of air where one cannot exist. The movement of air in the nose, mouth, and throat is nothing like a column on inhalation or exhalation. We could say it is column-like during its journey through the windpipe, but—as we're about to see—this would be the only place on the entire journey through the body that air acts like a column. Movement through the trachea is only a very small portion of the air's voyage through the body, and at less than five inches, it doesn't make for much of a column.

> **The movement of air in the nose, mouth, and throat is nothing like a column on inhalation or exhalation.**

Myth Buster

Playing with a more open throat results in a more resonant sound.

Why this myth has helped some people:

Many unnecessarily engage swallowing muscles when trying to take in a large quantity of air. Many oboe players unnecessarily tighten their neck muscles as they begin to play. A person with either of these habits may begin to release tension in the neck and/or throat when told to "open the throat," resulting in an improved tone.

How this myth is harmful:

Many do not create unnecessary tension in the neck or throat when playing the oboe. But hearing that an "open throat" improves the sound, they try to do something that they imagine feels like an open throat. This often creates tensions where none existed—in the back of the throat, the tongue, or other places throughout the body. Another danger inherent in the "open throat" myth is that the throat is seen as somehow controlling the breath.

Myth Replacement

A resonant sound is the result of natural and free breathing. An awareness of free neck and throat muscles allows air to flow in and out of the body through the movement of the ribs without interference from the swallowing muscles of the throat.

Research is being conducted to more accurately assess how changes in the pharyngeal space affect wind playing. Performers use movements of the tongue, soft palate, and possibly the glottis to impact tone quality and intonation or make it easier to produce pitches in extreme registers. Most players have no idea exactly what adjustments they make to the pharyngeal space in order to accomplish these things. Through trial and error they find what works for them. This can be compared to speech. Through trial and error we learn to speak clearly without noticing the specific movements of tongue, jaw, and soft palate that make this possible.

The Main Event: Ribs, Lungs, and Diaphragm

The respiratory system is complex and ingenious. Its primary purpose is to ensure that oxygen from the atmosphere reaches the bloodstream. Carbon dioxide is exhaled from the body as a byproduct of this activity. The vital infusion of oxygen into the blood is processed by the lungs and heart, both located in the chest cavity, sometimes called the thorax or thoracic cavity.

The thoracic cavity includes the thoracic spine, made up of the twelve thoracic vertebrae, each with ribs attached to both sides. Most of these ribs connect in the front to the sternum (the breastbone). The large diaphragm muscle connects to the bottom ribs. The twelve thoracic vertebrae, twenty-four ribs, sternum, and diaphragm form the boundaries of the thoracic cavity. As we'll soon see, these boundaries are never fixed, but constantly moving—down and up, out and in.

The functioning of the whole complex respiratory system depends on these movements of the thoracic cavity. These movements take place in two phases: inspiratory, which allows air to enter; and expiratory, which releases the air back out.

Understanding how the ribs move and the spine gathers and lengthens has the most direct effect on controlling the breath for oboe playing.

Inspiration consists of movements of the spine, ribs, and sternum, due mainly to the contractions of the diaphragm and the intercostal muscles of the ribs. These movements increase the size of the thoracic cavity.

Expiration also consists of movements of the spine and ribs, involving work by abdominal and intercostal muscles as well as release of the diaphragm. These movements bring the thoracic cavity back to a neutral state.

The lungs, connected to the ribs, respond to these thoracic movements. When the volume of the lungs is increased, air pressure is momentarily decreased. Since atmospheric pressure outside the body is now relatively higher, more air immediately enters the lungs. In expiration, lung volume decreases, which increases its air pressure. Air pressure in the lungs is now above that of the atmosphere, so air is forced out of the lungs.

Remember the statement above that respiration is complex and ingenious? Don't worry if all of this seems too complicated. As you continue reading and looking at the accompanying figures, it will become more clear. The important point for now—and it is important, in fact, crucial to playing the oboe—is that the primary movements of breathing are in the chest cavity. Oboe players must experience breathing as movements of the spine and ribs that coordinate with the lungs.

Presently, wind instrument teachers do not put enough emphasis on this primacy of movements in the thoracic cavity. Rather, they focus on the secondary things that respond to these primary movements (like movements of abdominal and pelvic muscles). This is like a bird focused on moving its tail feathers when flying but forgetting to flap its wings. Understanding how the ribs move and the spine gathers and lengthens has the most direct effect on controlling the breath for oboe playing.

The Lungs

Figures 10.2–3 help us clearly map the structure, function, and size of the lungs. The two lungs fill most of the thoracic cavity. You can see that the left lung is slightly smaller in front, allowing room for the heart. The top of each lung projects just above the first rib. Also notice how much space there is for air in the back of the lungs. Notice where the front of the spine is, and how much of the lungs are behind the weight-bearing spine.

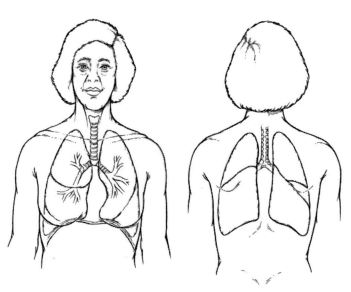

Figure 10.2. Lungs

Figure 10.2 also shows how air completes its journey to the lungs. The bottom of the trachea branches into two sections called *bronchi.* Each *bronchus* (the singular form of bronchi) enters a lung and continues to branch into smaller tubes. This branching is referred to as the bronchial tree. Air is transferred from the smallest branches, called *bronchioles,* to microscopic sacs named *alveoli.* The alveoli exchange oxygen and carbon dioxide with blood vessels.

A healthy set of lungs has more than 300 million alveoli. Spread out, all these alveoli would cover half a tennis court.[9] When we breathe, air travels to the alveoli via the myriad branches of the bronchial tree, moving in all directions: up, down, sideways, backward, and forward, pretty much all at once. So the idea that we can fill our lungs in sections ("First, the bottom! then the middle! then for those really long phrases—the top!") is only a fantasy.

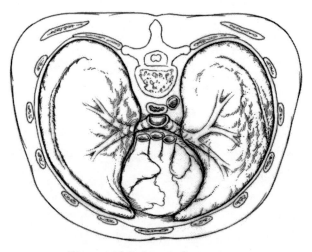

Figure 10.3. Lungs from above

The idea that we can fill our lungs in sections ("First, the bottom! then the middle! then for those really long phrases—the top!") is only a fantasy.

On exhalation, air leaves the body through the same pathways. From millions of alveoli, air molecules wind through the multitudinous branches of the bronchial tree, arrive at a bronchus and trachea, then whirl forward through the throat, finally exiting either the open mouth, or nose. This turbulence is nothing like the imagery suggested by many teachers: a sturdy column of air stretching from the lower torso to the reed.

The Ribs

Figure 10.4 shows the ribcage. Another unfortunate term, ribcage. The word "cage" implies something very stable and fixed. But "caged" means a loss of freedom. Ribs are not fixed, and their movements can be very free. When people think of ribs as a ribcage, they tend to think all the ribs move as a unit, which is also untrue.

There are twenty-four ribs, twelve on each side. Since the two sides mirror each other, we'll study just one side. The two bottom ribs are called floating ribs because they do not connect to anything in the front. They can move quite freely and function mainly to provide attachments for the diaphragm. The other ten ribs connect to the sternum in the

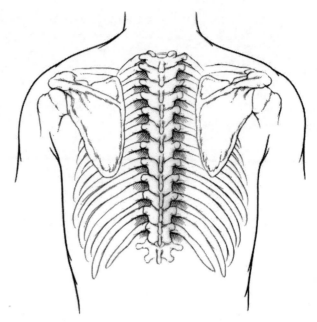

Figure 10.4. Ribs as seen from the back

front. This connection is made with flexible cartilage which increases the elasticity of the thoracic cavity. The first seven ribs each have a direct connection to the sternum, and are called *true ribs*. Ribs 8, 9, and 10 connect indirectly with the sternum, sharing cartilage with the seventh rib. Therefore ribs 8–12 are called the *false ribs*. Notice other differences between the ribs. The top ribs are quite small and round. Looking downward, the other ribs are progressively larger and more elliptical, gradually slanting more and more. The variations in size, shape, and slant result in a variety of possibilities for rib movement. The false ribs can move more than the true ribs, and the floating ribs have the most mobility.

Rib movement is possible mainly because of how the ribs are connected in the back. Each of the ribs is connected to the spine in the back, forming twenty-four joints with the spine. These are truly our "breathing joints."

Bach may move your soul; but to play Bach, you have to move your ribs!

Understanding the bony structures of the ribs won't fully explain how ribs move. Muscles move bones. The muscle primarily responsible for rib movement is the diaphragm. It accomplishes about seventy-five percent of the muscular work involved in respiration. Most of the rest of the work is done by intercostal muscles, found in the spaces between the ribs.

On inhalation, actions of the diaphragm and intercostal muscles cause the ribs to pivot slightly at their joints with the spine. The ribs are then raised. This movement is similar to lifting a bucket handle. Different ribs move in slightly different ways. In order to bring in a lot of air, the ribs move differently than they do to bring in a little air. Raising the ribs increases the overall circumference of the thoracic cavity. The more the ribs move, the more air will come in.

Moral of the story: Bach may move your soul; but to play Bach, you have to move your ribs!

Myth Buster

One must lift the sternum high in order to take a big breath.

Why this myth has helped some people:

Some are so focused on "breathing from the belly" that the upper body gets quite stiff, and rib movement is compromised. The instruction to keep the shoulders down when inhaling often exacerbates the problem. The metaphor of a ribcage is no help, either. When asked to raise the sternum, most begin to get more mobility from the ribs and take in more air.

How this myth is harmful:

It's quite easy to move the sternum up without affecting the breath at all. This is accomplished by thrusting the lumbar spine forward, or by bending back the thoracic spine. Either movement takes one off-balance and inhibits a deep connection to the pelvic floor.

Myth Replacement

Ribs sweep up and out on inhalation. On exhalation, they gradually move back down and in. Take a big breath, and the ribs move up and out a lot. The sternum, connected to the ribs, will move up naturally, in tandem with this rib movement. This is sometimes referred to as a deepening (front to back) of the chest cavity. Since the arm structure rests above the ribs, really big breaths may move the arm structure up a little as well, and this is okay.

The Diaphragm

The diaphragm is the very large muscle that separates the thoracic cavity from the abdominal cavity. It is attached to the ribs and spine. The diaphragm is a double dome, with the right dome larger than the left. When this muscle contracts it moves downward and its shape flattens out somewhat. It releases upward, returning to a more domed shape. The diaphragm's primary function is to increase the

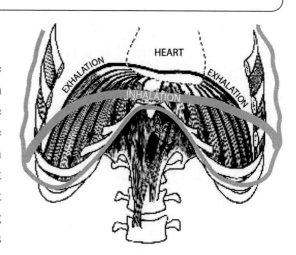

***Figures 10.5.** Diaphragm*

circumference of the thoracic cavity, causing air to flow into the lungs. The diaphragm's descent helps the ribs to move up and out, causing inhalation. Its ascent moves ribs back down and in, resulting in exhalation.

We can't feel the diaphragm's movement directly the way we sense muscles in the arms, because, like the heart, it doesn't contain kinesthetic receptors. But we can feel it indirectly. We feel movements responding to the contraction and release of the diaphragm: movements of the ribs, abdominal wall, and pelvic floor.

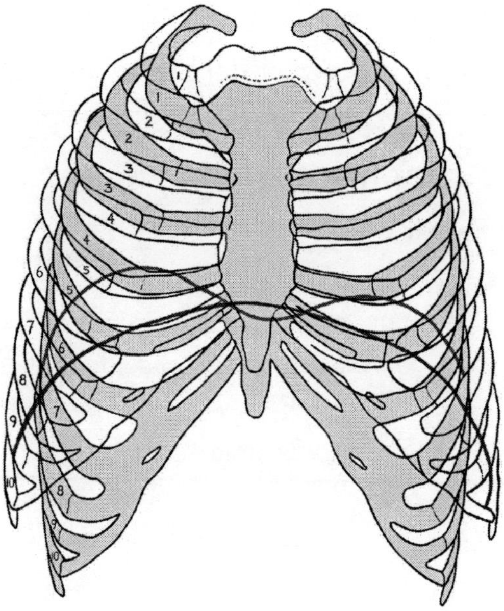

Figure 10.6. *Ribs and diaphragm*

Supporting Players—Muscles of the Abdominal Cylinder and Pelvic Floor

The muscles of the abdomen are not only in the front. They are also on the sides and in the back. The strong downward movement of the diaphragm muscle on inhalation pushes against the viscera in the abdominal area. Viscera are pushed down and away in all directions. I like to refer to the muscles of this area as the abdominal cylinder rather than the abdominal wall. There's not just one wall of muscle in front. The entire abdominal region is lined with muscles that respond to movements of the thorax. On exhalation, the abdominal musculature assists the diaphragm in its return. The abdominal cylinder recoils inward as pressure from the viscera is gradually reduced by the ascent of the diaphragm.

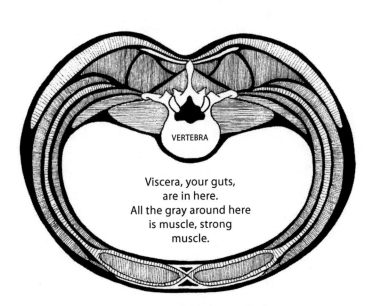

VERTEBRA

Viscera, your guts, are in here. All the gray around here is muscle, strong muscle.

Figure 10.7. *Abdominal cylinder*

The movement of the abdominal cylinder is a natural, involuntary response to the action of the diaphragm. It is not something we have to make happen; we simply allow it to happen. It should never feel like work.

If it's so natural, why do we have to consciously understand it? Unfortunately, many mis-map the movements of breathing. They imagine one breathes from the belly, or that the abdominal muscles should be rigid when playing, among other things. But even musicians who haven't mis-mapped breathing will find it helpful to become more aware of the

The movement of the abdominal cylinder is a natural, involuntary response. It should never feel like work.

coordination of rib movements with those of the abdominal cylinder. Studies have proven that coordination of the ribs and abdomen deteriorates during stressful situations.[10] Musicians are constantly expected to perform well in stressful situations. We avoid this common deterioration by working in the practice room on increasing our awareness of the coordination of movements of the ribs and diaphragm with the abdominal cylinder.

It's very easy to stick your stomach in and out. And unfortunately, some who are told to "breathe from the belly" end up doing just this. They move the stomach out without having any impact on the lungs. Some are told to control exhalation by pulling in the abs. This also can result in a lot of work with little effect on the air. Instead, let go of excess tension in the abdominal region and allow these muscles to respond to breathing with a natural dynamic rebound or recoil.

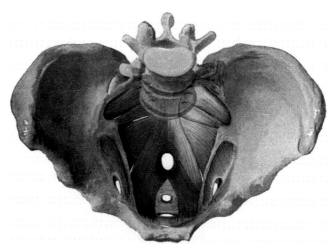

Figures 10.8. Muscles of the pelvic floor

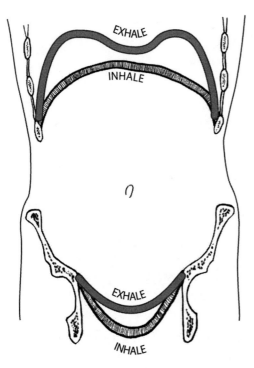

Figure 10.9. The two diaphragms

There are also many muscles below the viscera. The muscles of the pelvic floor respond to the diaphragm's movements. The viscera gently push downward against the pelvic floor musculature when the diaphragm descends. The ascent of the diaphragm releases the pressure against the viscera and the pelvic floor springs back up in response. Thus the muscles of the pelvic floor mirror the movement of the diaphragm. For this reason, the sling of muscles that cover the pelvis are sometimes referred to as the pelvic diaphragm.

These movements should also happen naturally; they should never be forced.

When the body is locked at the hip joints or is chronically out of balance at the lumbar spine, the pelvic floor's natural resilience is inhibited, and its response to diaphragm movements is limited. Attention to balance is crucial in order to release the pelvic floor, allowing a natural, dynamic rebound and recoil.

Some don't notice the actions of the pelvic floor muscles because they have not developed a kinesthetic connection to this area. Kegel exercises help with this. Kegels were developed for women preparing for childbirth and can be done by both men and women. In addition to improving awareness, Kegel exercises also improve muscle tone. To locate the proper muscles for Kegel exercises, simply stop urinating midstream. Kegel exercises consist of contracting these pelvic floor muscles for several seconds then releasing them slowly, repeating this ten times. As it gets easier, increase the amount of time these muscles are contracted.

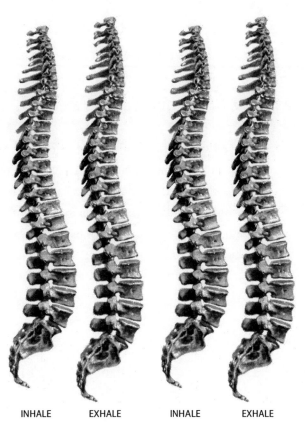

INHALE   EXHALE   INHALE   EXHALE

Figure 10.10. The gathering and lengthening spine

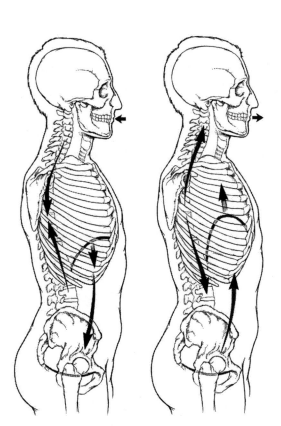

Figure 10.11. Coordinated breathing of a whole torso

Putting It All Together: The Spine

The spine coordinates the movements of breathing. The A-O joint at the top of the spine corresponds with the place where air comes into the body. Ribs, responsible for the movement of air, are directly attached to the spine. The spine's tailbone is aligned with the pelvic diaphragm.

Chapter 3 explains that the spine can gather and lengthen due to the plastic nature of the intervertebral discs. Spinal gathering and lengthening coordinates breathing. On inhalation, the spine gathers. The diaphragm's descent and the ribs' movements at joints along the spine are aided by the reflexive gathering of the spine. On exhalation, the spine lengthens. This lengthening accommodates the diaphragm's return and the ribs' movements back down and in.

81

The work involved in breathing is not effort, it is the work of setting right conditions so that the breath responds naturally to movements.

With good alignment, all the movements of breathing are free and effortless. The work involved in breathing is not effort, it is the work of setting right conditions so that the breath responds naturally to movements. There is no need to tense muscles in order to gain an artificial support for breathing. The term support is often used to talk about breathing for wind instruments, but what is meant by this? The dictionary defines support in two ways: "to hold up" and "to aid, or help." Sounds on the oboe are produced by sustained exhalation. Sustained exhalation is held up by a bony structure well-balanced over the floor or a chair; it is aided by the elastic recoil of the abdominal cylinder and pelvic floor and by the lengthening spine.

Therefore we can talk about five things that contribute to good breath support:

1. The body's bony structure
2. The floor or chair
3. The elastic recoil of the abdominal cylinder
4. The elastic recoil of the pelvic floor muscles
5. The lengthening spine

Epilogue: The Oboist's Paradox

This concludes the story of the breath's journey through the human body from top to bottom. Accurately mapping breathing makes performing more enjoyable. Respiration for oboists, like singers and other wind players, differs most from normal respiration on the exhalation. Ordinary exhalation is brief, regular, and mostly unconscious. For wind playing and singing, we control the exhalation in a slow, conscious manner that supports musical phrases.

The unique thing about oboe playing is that the reed doesn't allow the release of a large quantity of air. We always feel like we're holding back air. However, unless we play with high air pressure, the tone quality is unfocused, notes don't speak, and intonation suffers. So there's a paradox: we must act like we're releasing a lot of air even though the instrument makes us feel like we're holding our breath.

Let's consider this paradox in more detail. When it comes to oboe playing, what is the point of all these movements of breathing (the diaphragm and the abdominal and pelvic muscles in sync with a gathering and lengthening spine)? The point is to create the appropriate air pressure at the reed tip so that you can make beautiful music.

What is appropriate air pressure? This varies depending on the resistance of the reed used. But one can always gauge correct air pressure simply by listening to the quality of the sound produced. If you're producing a great sound, then you've found the proper air pressure. Obviously this takes some experimentation.

The oboe is an instrument that requires a relatively high air pressure but has a low flow rate. What does this mean? Flow rate is the quantity of air required to play a note on an instrument for one minute. This varies from instrument to instrument and changes due to range and dynamics. The oboe has the lowest flow rate of any wind instrument. "In *pianissimo* playing, the flow rate is about two and one-half liters per minute, and in *fortissimo,* would go up to about five liters per minute." The tuba, when playing *piano* uses about seven liters per minute and in *forte* can use up to 140 liters a minute. This information comes from *Arnold Jacobs: Song and Wind,* which documents the wonderful teaching of the former tuba player of the Chicago Symphony Orchestra revered as a teacher of breathing.[11]

A Word about Air Pressure

Air quantity, flow, and pressure are interrelated, as the following discussion will show. By definition, blowing air always involves all three. For this reason, most oboe players use the terms interchangeably, but usually have a preference for one or the other. Many wind players do not like using the term "air pressure," because pressure implies tension. They prefer to speak of "air speed." Others avoid "air speed" because this implies pushing or forcing the air in order to create speed. Although I use the term air pressure in this discussion, you may prefer to think air speed. Either one can be achieved with complete freedom.

To understand air flow, "Jacobs differentiates this as thin air and thick air. To show thin air, he has a student hold his hand in front of his mouth and say 'ssssss.' The air is under high pressure, but there is little quantity. Blow 'whoooooo' (as in who) for thick air. The feeling is a considerable volume of air under low pressure."[12]

It appears to me that the oboe, like brass instruments, requires a slightly lower air pressure with a higher flow rate in the low register. In the upper register the air pressure seems slightly higher with a lower flow rate. This difference is subtle, since the variation of air flow is so small on the oboe compared to other instruments; however, it is useful to recognize that this subtle difference exists.

Blow air at the high pressure needed to create a good sound on the oboe and you will feel a bit of a tug on the inner abdominal wall and from the pelvic floor. This is similar to the feeling one has when coughing or sneezing. It's helpful to pretend

> We must act like we're releasing a large quantity of air with as much muscular freedom as possible.

to cough or sneeze and notice which deep muscles are recruited. This is a sensation initiated from the inside, not the outside.

You can then use this same energetic air pressure to create a ringing, focused sound on the reed alone. If your reed is well made it should crow octave C's. You should play the reed as if the oboe were attached, using the same embouchure you use when playing oboe. Then play a *forte* C with as ringing, rich, and focused a sound as possible. If you can do this, then you probably are using the appropriate air pressure.

As you experiment with finding just the right air pressure to be able to play this focused and ringing pitch on the reed, choose a method that doesn't involve any strain. The neck muscles must be free, the throat clear, and the breath should seem to move instantly and effortlessly. I sometimes think of the movement of those deep interior muscles actually triggering the tongue and breath. I time the release of the tongue precisely with the moment of that tug in the lower abdominal region which initiates the breath. This usually results in a clear and effortless sound. This same type of blowing should translate into a beautiful sound when the oboe is attached to the reed.

So this explains the first part of our paradox. We must act like we're releasing a large quantity of air with as much muscular freedom as possible.

Now let's consider the second part of the paradox: feeling like we're always holding our breath.

Oboe players should experience just how little air it takes to play the instrument. Try exhaling every last ounce of air out of your body. Don't worry, no matter how hard you try to get rid of everything, your body always maintains a reserve of air, so you won't die! Once you feel like you've gotten rid of every last milliliter of air, then start playing the oboe. You'll be surprised by how long you can still play (flute players are *so* jealous!). You can also time yourself hissing "ssssss" after a big breath (how many seconds can you go?), then take the same amount of breath and play a note on the oboe. You will be able to play the note longer than you could hiss, for even hissing takes more air than playing the oboe does!

Many oboe players take in more air than they really need. Taking too much air can feel uncomfortable and interfere with good music making. Of course, not taking enough air to sustain a healthy tone throughout the length of the phrase is also a problem. It takes practice to develop an accurate sense of precisely the right amount of air needed to sustain a musical phrase. But this is an important skill that oboe players must develop.

Although we have enough breath to play long phrases, when we hold the breath for *very* long phrases, then carbon dioxide accumulates in the bloodstream. This is called *hypoventilation* (the opposite of hyperventilation). We need more oxygen, so our body asks for more breath even though the lungs are full of air. This is the uncomfortable feeling one can get playing the Strauss *Concerto,* which features successions of endless melody with very few rests.

One method to avoid hypoventilation was taught by Arnold Jacobs. "Jacobs has a student do three or four deep inhalation/exhalation cycles before a long phrase in an unobtrusive manner, just as a swimmer might do prior to prolonged activity underwater. This will decrease the carbon dioxide level temporarily delaying the body's need for the next breath. Then they take a full breath to play the phrase."[13]

By hyperventilating in this fashion, one then starts a passage with an increased oxygen level in the blood stream, which allows playing a long passage without the brain signaling the respiratory system to breathe.[14]

Oboists should also learn to take advantage of the ability to continue making a sound after exhaling. In order to relieve the back pressure one feels from having too much air, the oboe player must be equally comfortable with playing after inhaling or exhaling. Sometimes it's helpful to very quickly exhale, and then inhale between phrases (see figure 10.12). Rolf Julius Koch's *The Technique of Oboe Playing* includes numerous exercises for developing these techniques. Use the same suggestions given in figure 10.12 when practicing them.

An oboe player who is comfortable playing after inhaling or exhaling learns to look carefully at a musical score to determine which phrases should be played after inhaling, which after exhaling, or when it might be best to breathe through the nose or through the mouth. This sort of musical preparation is the most valuable way to deal with the oboist's paradox. Then we can breathe with freedom and ease, creating sounds the music demands, without succumbing to the resistance of a demanding instrument.

Playing Like a Pig

The soft palate, also known as the *velum,* forms the back part of the roof of the mouth. Unlike the rigid hard palate that forms the front part, the soft palate is capable of movement. One can easily feel this movement by saying "innng—ah." When phonating "innng" you will feel the soft palate against the back of the tongue. As you say "ah" you will feel the soft palate move up and away from the tongue.

Singers spend time learning to accurately feel the movement of the soft palate, and many oboe players do as well. Some oboists feel that the soft palate should be arched high in the mouth. This may improve resonance, ease articulation, and free the movement of air to the reed.

When the soft palate arches up, its muscular fibers seal off the passageway between the mouth and nose. This is useful for wind players because air pressure is directed toward the reed instead of escaping into the nose. However, many players have experienced what happens when the soft palate doesn't completely seal off this passageway. This leaking of air into the nose can cause a very unmusical grunting, and can be severe enough to prevent one from playing altogether. It often happens with young players who suddenly increase the number of hours they rehearse. It can also happen when one is sick, or as a result of using certain medications, especially ones that dry out the sinuses. Sometimes this happens because a player is using a reed with too much resistance. In many cases, the grunting is a result of poor breath management. Once the student sorts out how oboe players should manage the breath, the grunting stops.

There is a fancy name for this leaking of air into the nasal passages. It is referred to as "velopharyngeal incompetence," or "velopharyngeal stress insufficiency." Players who suffer from this on a regular basis should consult with an ear, nose, and throat specialist. Often simple exercises can be prescribed to alleviate this condition. In rare cases, surgery is required.

Circular Breathing

Circular breathing can be a lifesaver for an oboe player. This is the ability to press air from the oral cavity, using a combination of tongue and face muscles, while simultaneously breathing through the nose. It is possible to maintain a steady tone while either inhaling or exhaling through the nose. Just a small sniff of air can make a huge difference in relieving the back pressure oboists feel when playing very long musical phrases. There are also many pieces in the repertoire now that require this specialized technique.

I won't teach circular breathing here, because there are several other good resources available for learning it. But I will share a few refinements I've discovered since studying Body Mapping. The most important thing is to have a whole body awareness while circular breathing. With good alignment and a free neck, everything coordinates more easily.

Be careful to properly map where the air enters and leaves during circular breathing. The nose has two openings in front—the *nares,* commonly called nostrils. Air enters the nostrils and then passes through the nose, or nasal cavity. At the back of the nasal cavity are two apertures, called *choana* (plural, *choanae*), which lead air to the *nasopharynx.* For the purpose of circular breathing, you want to work with the air already in the nasal cavity at the choanae. If you bring in air with the nostrils you are working too hard. If you exhale at the nostrils, you are definitely working too hard. Working with the air at the back of the nasal cavity is easier and significantly quieter.

When learning circular breathing, many focus on the nose and the oral cavity. But in order to smoothly accomplish this unusual breathing technique it is also helpful to notice the ribs. During circular breathing the natural downward movement of the ribs is temporarily suspended while cheek muscles take over the work of expelling air. How do you inhale at this precise moment? The same way you always inhale: increase the overall size of the thorax by moving the ribs up and out. This is the only time the ribs move in an upward direction while you are producing a sound!

Adding the ribs to your awareness should make circular breathing feel more natural. Be certain you are not just moving the sternum up without actually lifting the ribs. In order to avoid this, think of moving the back of your ribs; then the air will easily be drawn in.

Body Mapping Practice 4

Air

Oboe playing should be an extension of normal, healthy breathing. To help accomplish this, here's another variation of our warm-up exercise. This time each phrase is repeated.

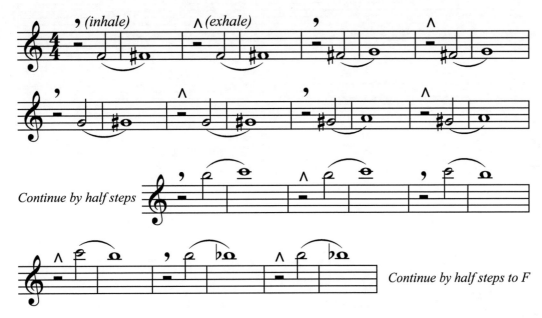

Figure 10.12. *Warm-up exercise*

1. First play after inhaling, then repeat the phrase after exhaling
2. The goal is to sound just as good after exhaling as you sound after inhaling
3. Play the repetition at the same dynamic level with the same resonance, start, and finish
4. At first, practice exhaling only a small amount of air, then experiment with exhaling a lot of air

Can you still play the oboe with almost no air in your lungs? You will find that you can. But can you play beautifully, with complete freedom and control, after exhaling a lot of air? You will find that, with practice, you can.

You should become proficient taking breaths through the mouth, and through the nose.

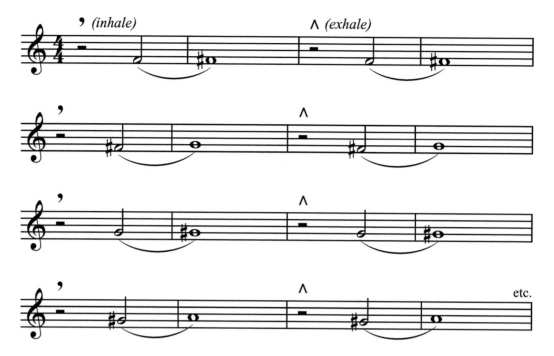

Figure 10.13. *Breathing exploration*

Practice this warm-up with the following conditions:

1. Always play with the most beautiful tone possible
2. Maintain an awareness of core balance (initiated with Alexander's orders)
3. Have complete kinesthetic awareness of the breathing movements when playing:
   a. Inhale using the breathing joints of the ribs
   b. Notice the gathering of the spine and the response of the pelvic floor
   c. While exhaling, notice:
      1. The rebound of the pelvic floor
      2. The ribs' movement down and in
      3. The lengthening of the spine (are the neck muscles free?)

Oboe players must make choices about inhalation and exhalation. How much should the ribs move for inhalation? This depends on how long the phrase is as well as reed resistance. Over time, oboists develop a sense of how much rib movement is needed to accommodate a particular musical phrase. While exhaling, at what rate do you need to move the ribs down and in? This is always determined by the quality of the sound—you want to sustain a consistently beautiful resonance all the way to the end of a phrase. If you've taken a full breath, the rate of rib movement needed to maintain a beautiful sound will seem quite slow at first. But toward the end of a phrase (especially a very long phrase), you may have to consciously move the ribs faster. For some, this movement must be matched by a conscious freeing of the neck muscles in order to accommodate spinal lengthening. When playing figure 10.13, you can simulate this feeling of being at the end of your breath during a very long phrase by exhaling a lot of air before repeating each phrase.

Once you become comfortable playing this warm-up you can use what you've learned about how the natural movements of breathing can support oboe playing in real life situations, such as this one:

Oboe playing should be an extension of normal, healthy breathing.

Figure 10.14. J. S. Bach, Cantata No. 56

The exhalation indicated in measure 4 must be accomplished quickly and quietly. The next inhalation should be large and feel quite free. If you have really moved your ribs down during the previous measure, your body will really want this breath and open up to it quite easily. This inhalation will support the long phrase that follows. There must be enough air to comfortably open up to a ringing high C, ending joyfully, not sounding weak and out of breath. Developing the ability to play this melody with ease is particularly important, since it is repeated numerous times during the aria. According to Bach's text for this aria, this oboe melody represents a person's soul, soaring like an eagle above the earth.

Chapter 11

Case Study Number 3: Ann's Surprise

The e-mail address is oboeismylife@earthlink.net, so I know this stranger and I have something in common. She's a student, living in a different part of the country and studying with a very good oboe teacher. Her name (fictitious) is Ann. She explains that about a year ago she was getting a lot of pain in her forearms. A doctor had ruled out medical issues, so her teacher suggested she take a Body Mapping course that was offered locally. Ann took this course and found it very helpful. She discovered she played with unnecessary ulnar deviation, so she worked hard to change how she used her hands when playing the instrument. She purchased a Kooiman thumb rest. She saw some improvement, but continued to worry because the pain would sometimes come back. She asked me if there was some other device she could purchase that might help her even more. I wrote back, suggesting that the best device she could use is her own brain, and encouraged her to continue her study of the body and how its movements affect her oboe playing. About a month later I got another e-mail from Ann. She was planning to visit family that lives nearby. Would I be willing to give her a lesson?

We met, and as I watched and listened to her playing Barrett, I noticed her hands and forearms looked quite good in relation to the instrument. Ann showed no signs of ulnar deviation, and seemed to be adjusting well to playing with the new thumb rest. The Barrett etude sounded very well practiced, but without much life. Likewise her dark oboe tone sounded constricted and held back. As I continued to watch Ann, I noticed her shoulders were locked most of the time and her breathing was labored. I heard her throat constricting every time she took a breath.

I asked if she heard how noisy her breathing sounded. No, she didn't notice. I asked if she knew why someone's breathing might be noisy. She remembered the Body Mapping course she took had related noisy breathing to tightening muscles in the throat. But she didn't think she had this problem. "I always try to keep my throat open when I play, so that I get a good sound," she told me.

But thinking that she must keep her throat open is exactly what was keeping her from playing at a higher level. In order to clear up this critical misconception, I talked to Ann about breathing. I spent a bit of time showing her pictures of the throat, ribs, and lungs. I found out that Ann was so focused on keeping her throat open as she plays that she didn't pay much attention to what was happening below her neck. I asked her to use her hands to touch her ribs. I then asked her to move her ribs toward her hands, to push her hands away. She did this with her mouth closed. Air entered through her nose as her ribs pressed against her hands.

"Did your ribs move toward your hands when you asked them to?" I queried.

"Yes," she answered.

"Did you notice air coming into your body as this happened?"

"No."

"Then please do the same thing again. With your hands on your ribs, ask the ribs to move toward your hands. Have your mouth closed as you do this, and notice if air comes into your nose."

Ann followed my instructions and did notice air moving through the nasal cavities as the ribs moved. I asked her to repeat the process one more time, this time with her mouth open.

"Be sure to focus mostly on the ribs moving against your hands." I watched her take air in noiselessly through her mouth.

"How did that feel?" I asked.

"That's the easiest breath I've ever taken!" she said, smiling.

"So that felt different than your normal oboe breaths?" I questioned further.

"Absolutely," she replied.

"And how did your throat feel, as the breath came in?" I wanted to know.

"It didn't seem like it was doing anything," was her answer.

Then I asked her to take her oboe reed and imitate some of the sounds I made with my oboe reed. I played a C on my reed, using lots of air, making a free, ringing sound. Ann matched the C pitch, but her sound was much smaller and weaker than mine. I encouraged her to let go with her air and really do whatever it takes to match my sound.

As she prepared to try again, she took a big breath in her old manner. This time, though, she noticed the sucking sounds she made as she inhaled. She laughed, "I better try that again." She then took a big breath noiselessly, using her ribs to initiate the inhalation. She used more air pressure this time, and got a much more ringing sound from the reed. Progress!

I asked Ann to blow into the reed in the same way, this time with the reed attached to the oboe. She played the Barrett etude, but sounded completely different. I heard a forward-moving phrase with a rich, resonant sound. I also saw that her shoulders were no longer locked at her sides. When Ann stopped playing, she said excitedly, "My arms feel so free when I let go of the air!"

Agenda Helper **5**

Air

Mark the statements that are true for you. Work on the ones that aren't checked.

- ❑ I breathe fully and without strain.
- ❑ I allow my spine to gather as I inhale and lengthen as I exhale.
- ❑ I feel a wonderful support from the whole of me as I play.
- ❑ Basically I can do whatever I want when I play.
- ❑ I always have all the air I need.
- ❑ I always use the air I have fully and efficiently.
- ❑ I'm skilled at matching the air I take in to the phrase I am going to play.
- ❑ I easily begin my breath.
- ❑ I easily end my breath.
- ❑ I clearly perceive the movement of my breathing.
- ❑ My breathing feels dynamically supported.
- ❑ I use the information coming to me from my nasal passages as I inhale.
- ❑ I allow my diaphragm its full excursion up and down.
- ❑ I use the information coming to me from my mouth as I inhale and exhale.
- ❑ I open my jaw with ease.
- ❑ I close my jaw with ease.
- ❑ My neck is free as I play.
- ❑ My throat is free as I play.
- ❑ My ribs move appropriately as I play.
- ❑ I am free of heaving as I play.
- ❑ I understand my rib movement, and I can change my rib movement when I need or want to.
- ❑ I know right where my lungs are, and I can fill them fully if I need or want to.
- ❑ I play with my whole body.
- ❑ I allow my abdominal wall full freedom in playing so that I don't interfere with the full excursion of my ribs and diaphragm.
- ❑ I allow my pelvic floor full freedom in playing so that I don't interfere with the full excursion of my ribs and diaphragm.

Chapter 12

The Tongue

I once heard a finely tongued passage described as a string of little pearls.
Bad tonguing belongs in the chicken yard rather than in the jewellery shop!
Think musically. Use the tongue as a fine string player uses the bow.

Evelyn Rothwell[15]

The Language of Articulation

When we speak of articulation or tonguing, we mean more than just playing a lot of fast staccato notes. For wind players, tonguing is the essence of a good sound—every note begins with an articulation. It is also a key factor in creating a variety of musical colors. One would think something so essential to the basic tone of the instrument would be the subject of endless analysis; but the secrets of wind articulation are a mystery that most teachers shroud in confusion.

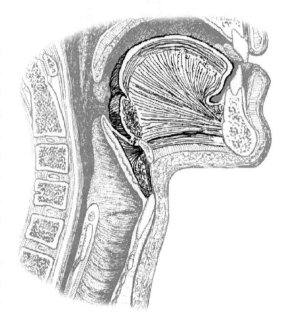

This chapter explores some of the language traditionally used by wind players to work with tonguing problems and how it is inadequate in many cases. It also presents some new vocabulary that helps solve articulation problems: a new vocabulary for instrumentalists using language itself as its basis.

Many oboe teachers talk about articulation and focus solely on the sound the student should strive for with little attention paid to the physical methods for producing these sounds. Teachers giving verbal descriptions and playing demonstrations of legato, staccato, marcato, *détaché,* etc., leave students wondering how to recreate these styles in their own playing. This chapter explains the muscular movements responsible for making a wide variety of articulations and gives suggestions about how to practice these movements to improve accuracy and gain speed.

To fully understand articulation, one must map the breathing mechanisms with great detail, paying special attention to the tongue, throat, jaw, and face. The throat, jaw, and face are discussed in more detail in chapters 9 and 10. This chapter discusses mapping the tongue.

Some oboe players haven't developed a kinesthetic awareness of the movements of the tongue. They don't notice how these movements contribute to articulation. But awareness of the tongue's movements is beneficial, not just for creating a variety of articulation styles, but also for creating a good, basic oboe sound and a varied tonal palette.

When watching dance, whether ballet or hip-hop, we enjoy performers who are buoyant, who seem to spring effortlessly from one movement to the next. Start noticing and enjoying the dance of the tongue on the reed as you play the oboe. The tongue, like a good dancer, should also be buoyant and spring effortlessly from one movement to the next. You can choreograph the movements of the tongue in a way that immediately brings to life the music you hear in your head. Good dancers are very aware of the limits of what their muscles can do and work hard to achieve an efficiency of movement that results in effortless performance. Likewise, oboists need to understand the capabilities of the muscles related to articulation, particularly the tongue muscle, in order to improve the efficiency of articulation in performance.

> To fully understand articulation, one must map the breathing mechanisms with great detail, paying special attention to the tongue, throat, jaw, and face.

Students are often concerned about achieving a fast staccato with both single and double tonguing. This chapter deals quite a bit with this issue, but with the following understanding: although an artist's mastery of articulation may be more obvious in a solo like Rossini's *La Scala di Seta*, infamous for its treacherous string of staccato notes covering a two-octave compass, mastery of articulation is every bit as necessary to produce the seamless legato line needed in Tchaikovsky's *Symphony No. 4*.

Some discussions about articulation only focus on the way a tone is initiated with the tongue. However, one must also be aware of how to end a sound. The method for ending a sound often becomes the setup for the initiation of the next sound. For this reason articulation is more than just "tonguing"; it is intimately connected to embouchure and air. As John Mack states:

> Instead of putting the tongue against the reed, you must learn to allow the tongue to return to the reed *with the wind....* Learn to allow your tongue to go back with the wind so you can play a line that has the constancy and value of a legato line but with articulation, even with massive spaces between the notes.[16]

Some oboists advocate a relatively fixed embouchure in order to best articulate. The danger of this is that the embouchure can become immobile. Chapter 9 gives many details about the muscles of the face and the formation of embouchure, but here is a brief summary:

1. An embouchure involves many face muscles moving with the jaw and interacting with air and the reed in order to find the appropriate sound for a musical passage.
2. It moves slightly differently for high notes than for low notes.

3. The embouchure responds to intonation problems, making slight adjustments to bring a note in focus.

4. It assists in making diminuendos and crescendos and in creating the multitude of tone colors that make the oboe such an attractive instrument for so many players.

5. All this activity must coordinate with good articulation.

For this to happen, one must be clear about the structure and function of the jaw. The jaw should move with ease in order to coordinate with breath and tongue and make good music on the oboe. The various mis-mappings of the jaw discussed in chapter 9 can keep the jaw from moving with ease and undermine articulation. The jaw can work with the embouchure both for beginning and finishing a sound, whether it is short or long. Below there is a discussion of the relationship of

An oboe player's use of air has a profound effect on articulation.

diction to oboe articulation. It explains that the jaw also moves naturally with the tongue in order to make certain consonant sounds related to oboe articulation.

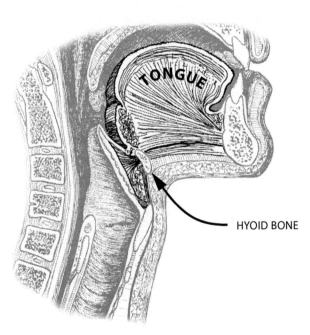

HYOID BONE

Figures 12.1. The tongue

An oboe player's use of air has a profound effect on articulation. The throat should be a free passageway for the movement of air. Without proper air pressure, tonguing at any speed can become strained and tone quality can suffer. Even the most rapidly tongued musical passagework should still sound musical. It needs life and direction, impossible to achieve without proper air pressure behind the sound.

The tongue needs to move freely and with great flexibility as it responds in a quick and uninhibited manner to the musical messages being sent by the brain. Gaining great kinesthetic awareness of the tongue at the reed is crucial to improving articulation.

Mapping the Tongue

Look closely at figure 12.1. First notice the size of the tongue. Many are surprised to see just how much of the oral cavity is filled up with the tongue. Notice how close it is to the hard and soft palate, making it easier to access the very quick movements needed to play *Midsummer's Night Dream* or *Scala di Seta*. This close proximity is a reason to develop an awareness of the soft palate, since a chronically lowered soft palate can inhibit free tongue movements.

Now notice that about two-thirds of the tongue muscle lies in the mouth, just below the hard and soft palate. Many are only aware of this part of the tongue. However there is more to the tongue than this portion in the mouth. The other third of the tongue faces toward the throat. This part of the tongue is actually the front of the throat. This is another reason we should avoid the phrase "play with an open throat." Many actually tense up the tongue muscle when attempting to "open their throats," thereby creating an array of articulation problems. Some players correctly map the tongue as being in the throat but mistakenly imagine a separate front of the throat lying behind the root of the tongue. This mis-mapping also greatly limits tongue movement.

Here we consider three sections of the tongue: the front (or tip), the back, and the root.

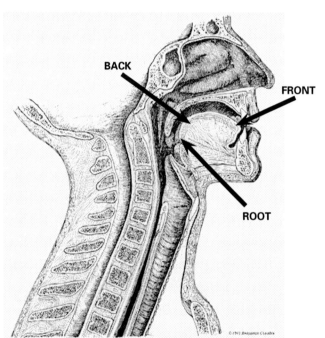

Figure 12.2. *The three sections of the tongue*

The tongue is connected at its root to the hyoid bone. Notice that the epiglottis (the upper part of the larynx) is connected to the other side of the hyoid bone.

The tongue is a unique muscle in the body. It appears to be just one large muscle, but in reality is a composite muscle. It's made up of several smaller muscles, both intrinsic and extrinsic, most with large multisyllabic names such as "pharyngoglossus." Now that's a mouthful! In other parts of the body muscles are separated by connective tissue, but the many muscles of the tongue are not. This allows for the complex movements involved in chewing, swallowing, saying words like "pharyngoglossus," and of course, playing the oboe.

Because of this unique structure we are able to move the front and back sections of the tongue independently. We can also move the whole tongue all at once. But we don't have to.

Many oboe players have tonguing issues because they have mapped the tongue as one big muscle and therefore attempt to articulate using the whole tongue. They also expect to feel the whole tongue working all the time. But single tonguing is best accomplished using only the tip of the tongue, and double tonguing uses the tip in alternation with the back. Double tonguing isn't possible if the tongue isn't mapped as a composite muscle (many muscles which can work independently of each other).

Myth Buster

The tongue is one muscle.

Why this myth has helped some people:

It hasn't. It's simply a misconception.

How this myth is harmful:

Trying to always use the tongue as a single muscle creates unnecessary tension, making articulation sluggish and dull.

Myth Replacement

Understanding the true structure of the tongue as a composite muscle allows us to access its free movements. This results in more precision of articulation with a great variety of tone shadings.

Finally, notice in figure 12.2 how the tongue is closely nestled together with the air passageways (oral and laryngeal pharynx, including the trachea and larynx), and how the thoracic spine is also close by. This is why it is so important to maintain a free neck if one wants to achieve a clear and free articulation.

Embouchure, Air, Tongue—Which Comes First?

Oboists have different approaches to starting a note. Most agree that the sound starts when the tongue comes away from the reed. It's often helpful for students to understand that even though many musicians speak of an articulation as an attack, oboe players will not get pleasant, musical results if they attack the reed with the tongue to start a sound. The tongue does go toward as well as away from the reed. But most oboists agree that for better control of a pleasant-sounding articulation, the player should focus on moving the tongue away from the reed, not going toward it. There is less agreement, however, on what exactly should happen before this. Some breathe, then set the embouchure, then set the tongue. Others set the embouchure, then set the tongue, then breathe, then remove the tongue from the reed. For some it's important that the breath be taken in tempo; others find this creates tension.

Arnold Jacobs, concerned with "locking" the breath, encouraged players to find a way to make articulation part of a natural cycle of inhalation and exhalation. He noticed a great deal of tension arose when wind players held the breath in order to set the embouchure and tongue before finally releasing the sound.

Joseph Robinson (former principal oboist of the New York Philharmonic) also suggests avoiding this when he asks oboe players to "exhale before playing."[17] Other oboe players advocate setting the air first: "breathe, hold, tongue in place, think pitch, release."[18]

The beauty of inclusive awareness (as discussed in chapter 2) is that it allows any of these approaches to work. *If* one is always conscious of core support and maintaining the balance of the skull at the A-O joint, one can accomplish any of these methods with ease. I agree with

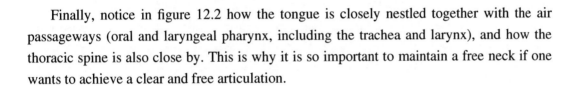

Jacobs that setting the breath often causes tension in wind players, but it doesn't have to. If players want to use this method (take in air and hold it while preparing the embouchure and tongue, then articulating), they can use it successfully if they stay in balance and continue to use their kinesthetic sense to monitor for a free neck.

Developing a Broad Range of Articulations

The achievement of a consistently beautiful sound on the oboe is such an art in itself that it has become the norm for good oboe players to be content with merely producing a refined, smooth, and even sound on every note at any speed. This seems to especially be true of the American school of oboe playing. Yet it was a great American oboe player, Ray Still, who opened me up to the idea that we should challenge the oboe to produce a great variety of beautiful articulation styles—equivalent to the tremendous variety of sounds great violinists achieve with the bow or great singers achieve through beautiful diction. One can hear Still's masterful approach to articulation in his recordings of the Bach *Cantata 202* and *Sonata in G Minor*, as well as many recordings he made as principal oboist of the Chicago Symphony Orchestra. Composers use a variety of symbols to indicate many types of articulated styles—several accent marks, dots, dashes, slurs, and combinations of these; and words like "legato tongue," marcato, staccato, etc. Though some of these indications refer mostly to the length of a note, often they also imply a certain style of articulation. Since Ray Still introduced me to the potential of articulation on the oboe I have spent a great deal of time developing this skill for myself and finding ways of teaching it to others.

Many oboe players talk about playing with a light tongue. Students who have trouble developing speed of articulation and those who tend to start every sound in an unrefined, non-musical manner are often helped by this concept of lightness in the tongue stroke. But in my quest to find a method for achieving variety in articulation, I have found that thinking only about lightening up is simply inadequate.

In fact, when people speak about tongue movement in terms of light and heavy, they are only reinforcing the false idea that the weight of the tongue is what causes changes in the sound. The differences between a tone with a beautiful and refined start as opposed to an ugly, blatty one, or a quick and lively staccato as opposed to one which is sluggish and dead-sounding have nothing to do with the weight of the tongue muscle. This weight is constant. No amount of mind games or articulation studies will change the amount a tongue weighs. Oboe players benefit when they get beyond the myth of lightness and heaviness and begin to understand in greater detail exactly how tongue movements relate to sound production.

> In my quest to find a method for achieving variety in articulation, I have found that only thinking about lightening up is simply inadequate.

But first let's explore why the myth of lightness seems to work for some players. One possibility is that tonguing problems stem from involving the whole tongue muscle unnecessarily. When players with this problem are told to lighten up, they begin using the front of the tongue muscle independently from the rest of the tongue. This makes the tongue feel lighter. Those who try to use the whole tongue for articulation will feel the tongue as heavy against the reed. The sound of the articulation will seem stiff and speed will be compromised.

Another possibility is that tonguing problems come from actually moving the tongue too far away from the reed. When students with this problem are told to lighten up, they begin keeping the tongue closer to the reed, making the distance traversed by the tongue shorter and the movement quicker. Again, the tongue seems to be less heavy.

And herein lies the problem with asking a student to lighten up. These are two very different problems with two different solutions. Isn't it more effective to give the student a specific goal ("use the front of the tongue," or "notice the distance your tongue moves away from the reed") rather than just saying "lighten up," and hoping the student figures it out?

Although we cannot change the weight of the tongue, there are things about it that we *can* change, and these can make a tremendous difference in how articulation sounds. We can change the speed at which the tongue withdraws from the reed as well as the speed at which it returns. We can also change the position of the tongue in the mouth as well as its placement against the reed. These oboemotions are key to becoming a good oboist.

Myth Buster

The terms light and heavy are an effective means for solving articulation problems.

Why this myth has helped some people:

Light and heavy can be used to describe the sound of an articulation. Some students mindlessly put tongue to reed without noticing the quality of the sound produced, content merely to reproduce notes on a page. The teacher opens the student's ear to how the sound being produced is inappropriate for the music: too heavy, too light. Awareness of the quality of sound being produced always leads toward improvement. When students open the ear to the light-heavy distinction in the sound, they will eventually stumble onto a tongue movement to achieve the sound goal.

How this myth is harmful:

The tongue itself is thought of as light or heavy. Teachers even speak of a light or heavy tongue when referring to articulation. But the tongue's weight does not change, and its weight has nothing to do with the quality of articulation. Using the terms light and heavy focuses attention on the tongue's weight against the reed, when it is the tongue's *movement* that should be monitored.

Myth Replacement

Monitoring the quality of the tongue's movement is the most effective way to solve articulation problems. In order to achieve the precise articulation the music requires, we can:

1. Vary the speed of the tongue's movement
2. Change the position of the tongue
3. Control the air expulsion created by the tongue's position and movement

The Tongue's Movement

Here's what I've discovered. I encourage you to experiment with these things yourself, using the musical examples below to help you in your explorations.

The movement of the tongue in articulation is essentially an up-and-down movement, not back-and-forth.

All tongue movements needed for good oboe playing rely on freedom in the neck and throat as well as lack of tension in the back of the tongue, so that the front of the tongue muscle moves independently with freedom and accuracy. I find it very helpful to think of tongue movement away from the reed as an up-and down rather than a back-and-forth motion. In reality, it is sometimes a little of both. However, many who think of the tongue moving back and forth tend to think of the *whole* tongue moving back and forth, which greatly hampers speed and accuracy. When asked to move the tongue up and down, most make the movement using only the front of the tongue, which of course is what should be encouraged.

Experiment for yourself.

1. Articulate a few notes, concentrating on the tongue moving back and forth.
2. How does the tongue feel as you do this?
3. How do the notes sound?
4. Now articulate a few notes, concentrating on the tongue moving up and down.
5. Does this feel different?
6. Does this sound different?

Although we cannot change the weight of the tongue, there are things about it that we can change, and these can make a tremendous difference in how articulation sounds.

For some players the difference in both sensation and sound will be profoundly different. Others will experience almost no difference. The results vary depending on the built-in habits each individual brings to oboe playing. Many students find this image of up-and-down tonguing especially useful in improving double tonguing skills.

At this point you should also begin to develop an awareness of the distance the tongue travels downward from the reed. Can you decrease the distance it presently moves? If so, you will find this to be an asset. Developing a quick return to the reed may allow you to increase the metronome setting by several numbers during practice.

The movement of the tongue affects the expulsion of air at the reed.

In order to gain control of a beautiful variety of sounds on the oboe, one must accurately map the tongue's movements at the reed. During practice sessions one must develop enough of a kinesthetic awareness of the tongue and its movements that one is sensitive to the tongue's placement in the mouth and on the reed as well as the speed of its movements and how these movements relate to air expulsion at the embouchure. This sounds like a lot of work and analysis. Fortunately, we don't have to get overly technical to understand these other movements. If you can talk, then you have been practicing these movements beautifully for years and have developed complete mastery over them. The tongue movements we use in speech are perfectly adequate for articulating music as well.

Speech is second nature for us, one of those habits that is so natural we are really not aware of how it works. So to take full advantage of it for oboe playing we must learn to gain conscious control of the speech movements which are most useful to articulation: the syllables [t], [d], and [l] for single tonguing, and [k] and [g] for double tonguing.

I have looked at many oboe method books from around the world, and these are the syllables most often mentioned. However, it's important to recognize that the manner of producing these sounds is not universal. The analysis that follows is a model based on American English. The drawings and technical descriptions are based on American diction. However, once the concepts of how personal diction relates to oboe articulation are understood, then the model can be adapted to other languages and even personal eccentricities. My hope is that oboe players find a variety of sounds used in their everyday language (whether Spanish, German, or Japanese) that can also be used to create a rich variation of oboe colors. What I've discovered is that in order to gain reliability and consistency, whatever sounds you decide to use must be understood in terms of placement and movement.

Diction books describe the syllables [t], [d], [k], and [g] as *plosives*.

The plosives are made by momentarily stopping the outgoing air stream, thus building up air pressure. The velum [soft palate] is raised, thereby preventing the escape of breath through the nose. Then the tongue is dropped or the lips opened suddenly, and the impounded air is released with a little explosion.[19]

[t] and [d] are both articulated in a similar manner:

1. *Place of articulation:* Tongue tip and upper gum ridge.
2. *Typical production:*

    The tongue is raised so that the tongue tip comes in contact with the upper gum ridge. The soft palate is raised to prevent nasal emission of breath. The sides of the tongue near the tip are in contact with the upper molars. The tongue, tense and extended, is held in this position for a fraction of a second. Then, quickly,

and as completely as possible, the tongue is retracted, with a resultant slight "explosion" of air at the tongue tip. This should be felt as a puff of breath if you hold your hand in front of your mouth.[20]

3. Usually the jaw moves as the tongue is retracted.

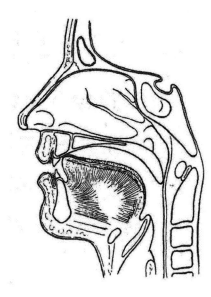

Figure 12.3. [t] and [d]

[l]:

In common with the alveolar stop sounds [t] and [d], the [l] is usually produced with the tongue tip in contact with the upper gum ridge. A difference, however, is that the blade of the tongue (the portion left and right just behind the tongue tip) is lowered and so permits vocalized breath to escape over the sides. The soft palate is raised to prevent nasal reinforcement and nasal emission. The result is a continuant and vowel-like quality that some phoneticians refer to as a liquid sound.[21]

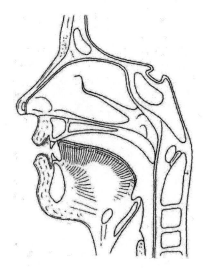

Figure 12.4. [i]

These descriptions allow us to accurately map the complex choreography of oboe tonguing, a skill we have already mastered in speech. The beauty of [t], [d], and [l] is that the tongue position is essentially the same for each. When speaking all three of these syllables the tip of the tongue is in contact with the upper gum ridge. Oboe players have the tip of the reed in a position that interrupts the tongue's contact with the gum ridge, so for oboe playing, the tongue hits the reed tip instead. Some people do articulate on the hard palate instead of the reed, but this does not give players as much control and limits the variety of articulation styles available to them.

Our guide must always be the quality of the sound merged with naturalness of technique.

For speech, [t] is defined as an unvoiced sound and [d] is a voiced sound. Obviously [d] is not voiced when playing the oboe, but we can take advantage of the difference in "explosiveness" of these two syllables.

[t] has a more explosive quality than [d]. Simply put the palm of your hand in front of your mouth to feel the difference as you say [t] and [d]. The [l] sound is made from a slightly different position. The sides of the tongue are not in contact with the upper teeth (as they are for the [t] and [d] sounds) and therefore some breath escapes over the sides, which makes the expulsion of air at the tongue tip quite minimal.

So we have one basic tongue position which is able to produce three very different sounds in speech: [t], [d], and [l]. The same use of the tongue results in three slightly different types of articulation for double reed players. The crucial thing to understand is that if the player is producing the appropriate air pressure for making a beautiful sound, then to create speech-like variations in the sound all one needs to do is use the tongue as described above.

Unfortunately, many oboe players involve more than the tongue in articulation. In an attempt to help out the tongue they involve the throat, abdomen, or embouchure more than necessary. If you have learned to produce a healthy sound, then the extra push of air provided by the tongue tip is enough to give you a beautiful variety of articulated nuances.

The idea of using consonant sounds as a basis of articulation is not new. In fact it is generally taught not only in the oboe world but for all wind instruments. What is different here is that I advocate a true understanding of the mechanics of diction in order to more accurately bring out a musical intention. Often teachers simply equate [t] and [d] with light and heavy. If a student is not articulating with enough clarity, then the teacher recommends using a [t]. If the student's tones are too brutal, then the teacher recommends a lighter approach—the [d]. The student then uses the [t] or [d] (whichever one worked for them) from then on as the basic way of initiating all sounds. I advocate greater flexibility. Depending on the musical effect you want to achieve, some tones start with [t], some with [d], and some even with other consonant sounds such as [l].

Many oboists pair these syllables with a vowel in order to maintain a somewhat consistent shape in the pharyngeal space: *ta, da, la; to, do, lo;* etc. Different vowel sounds alter the position and shape of the tongue in the pharyngeal space, so it is worth taking time to explore these different combinations of consonants and vowels in order to find the tongue position that is most comfortable for you and allows you to consistently produce a lovely tone.

Hard and fast rules can't be made for which consonant/vowel pairings work best. Individual tongue sizes and shapes vary, as do so many other factors involved in double reed playing, particularly related to the reed. How much reed is in the mouth certainly has an impact. Therefore our guide must always be the quality of the sound merged with naturalness of technique. One person feels the tongue should be high in the mouth and articulates using *du;* another wants the tongue low in the mouth, and articulates *tah*. Both can sound fantastic. But each will discover even more precise and varied articulations by noticing the tongue's position, size, and quality of its movements.

Many oboe players wonder exactly what part of the tongue should be touching the reed and exactly what part of the reed the tongue should touch. This also can vary a great deal from player to player, but generally somewhere near the tip of the tongue should be touching somewhere near the tip of the reed. "Somewhere near" can mean slightly above, slightly below, or directly at the tip.

[k] and [g] are usually used in conjunction with [t] and [d] for double tonguing. It's best to have a thorough understanding of single tonguing before adding the extra dance steps involved in double tonguing, so let's explore some other important issues related to the movements used for single tonguing.

The faster the tongue moves away from the reed, the greater the accent will be.

Experiment 1

- Do this on the reed alone, and then on the oboe.
- Become precise about how your tongue works in relation to starting a sound. Is your tongue touching the reed as you take a breath, before you begin a sound?
- Or is the tongue hovering somewhere just behind the reed as you take a breath, then touching the reed and quickly moving away at the moment of articulation?
- Or does it do some variation of either of these?

There are many possibilities for how the tongue movement coordinates with air intake. The point is that many oboe players don't know what they are doing. They just do something habitual, which may or may not be completely effective.

I find it useful to have the tongue tip already touching the reed and then to take in air, either through the nasal passages or mouth. Once enough air has been taken in, I then retract the tongue tip downward from the reed. This can all be done very quickly, either with or without holding (or setting) the air. Although I don't use this approach all the time, I do use it for the following exercises in order to gain a precise appraisal of how the speed of the tongue movement affects tone initiation.

Experiment 2

- With the tongue at or near the tip of the reed, use the front of the tongue muscle in a down-and-up motion to experiment with the difference in sound when varying the speed at which the tongue leaves the reed.
  - A very quick movement creates a highly accented sound.
  - A very slow movement creates a gentle articulation.
  - A medium movement achieves a start to the sound that is somewhere between highly accented and gentle.
- Both long tones or short staccato notes can be played with any of these three tongue speeds. Go ahead and try it!
- The length of a note is determined by how it is ended, not how it is begun. The speed at which the tongue leaves the reed is not related to a note's length; it only affects the way a note begins.

Please note that these three variations of tongue speed for beginning a sound can be achieved at any dynamic level. So now experiment with achieving the three different types of articulations at various dynamics and voila! This gives you an increased range of oboe colors far beyond the traditional two: light or heavy.

Experiment 3

- Do this on the reed alone, and then on the oboe.
- Notice the variation in tone quality created by using a *ta, to,* or *tu* articulation versus *da, do, du* or *la, lo, lu.*
- The difference between these articulations should be similar to the three accents achieved above, but more subtle.
- Now play these at different dynamic levels.
- Now combine the three movements developed in experiment 2 with the three syllables developed in experiment 3. In other words:
  - A fast movement of the tongue away from the reed with *ta, da,* then *la.*
  - A medium movement with *ta, da,* then *la.*
  - Finally, a slow movement with *ta, da,* then *la.*

You have just played nine different and easily definable types of articulation—a much wider spectrum than light and heavy! Now you can play all nine variations of articulation at different dynamic levels and access an even wider color spectrum!

As you experiment with these ideas, you'll find that certain articulations work better than others in particular registers of the instrument. Most oboists would agree that when it comes to articulation issues, one of the most difficult passages in the orchestral literature is actually a solo known for its beautiful legato line—the slow solo in Richard Strauss's *Don Juan.* It begins on a low D which must sound beautiful and placid and must be inflected as a pick-up note. For many oboe players this is an articulation issue every bit as stressful as playing the fast staccato passagework in Rossini's *La Scala di Seta*.

Figure 12.5. *Richard Strauss,* Don Juan, *solo*

For me, moving the tongue relatively slowly from the reed, but with *ta* allows the low D to sing appropriately. Using *ta* gives me more security in the low register where response is often an issue, especially under stress. But if I use *ta* with a fast tongue movement, then it sounds accented, which detracts from the upbeat feeling.

Oboists can plan articulations like violinists plan bowings. Here's a possible way to interpret the solo oboe part from the third movement of Berlioz's *Symphonie Fantastique*. I use a variety of articulations to bring out Berlioz's intentions as indicated in the score.

Figure 12.6. *Hector Berlioz,* Symphonie Fantastique, *offstage solo*

You could interpret the ethereal solo from Beethoven's *Symphony No. 3* in this manner:

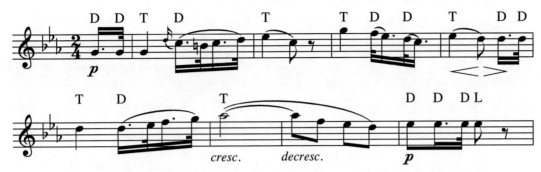

Figure 12.7. *Ludwig van Beethoven,* Symphony No. 3, *funeral march solo*

These are all experiments that allow your brain and body to create a greater variety of nuance. *I do not advocate analyzing every articulation of every solo in this manner.* Once these experiments are done your brain has a repertoire of sounds to choose from (like an artist chooses colors from a palette) and the body knows how to produce those sounds efficiently. Imagine the sounds and they will happen.

However, when you run into trouble, this knowledge of how the tongue's movements affect the tone may prove invaluable.

The End

All the information so far has been about how oboists start a sound. But what about ending a sound and setting up for the next one? The same information guides you in deciding how to best achieve this. Many outstanding musicians have very different approaches. Some stop the air, some say absolutely never stop the air. Some stop the sound with the tongue, others say never stop the sound with the tongue. Some use the embouchure.

Ray Still, like his teacher Robert Bloom, advocates using the embouchure to end a note no matter what the length of the note is. Still developed a variety of exercises that train one to successfully finish even very short notes by coordinating tongue, breath and embouchure. He played with amazingly free and flexible use of jaw and face muscles,

> Like the variety of ways we can start a note, with a correct mapping of the areas crucial to articulation, we can successfully end notes with a variety of methods as well.

and I believe this accounted for the colorful phrasing he accomplished (his superior ear and exceptionally creative musicianship certainly helped too!).

However, other oboe players firmly believe the embouchure should not be involved in ending a note. Stevens Hewitt in his *Method for Oboe* consistently warns against the "chewing gum embouchure." He writes, "The tongue is completely independent of wind and embouchure. *Nothing* moves except the tone."[22]

Like the variety of ways we can start a note, with a correct mapping of the areas crucial to articulation, we can successfully end notes with a variety of methods as well.

Tonguing on the Corner

Many oboists advocate placing the tongue on a corner of the reed (usually the right corner) in order to get a more fleet and better-sounding articulation. I am concerned about how one gets to the corner of the reed. Most methods have the reed in the mouth at a slight angle, which may inhibit the ability of the embouchure to shape the sound. Another method has the entire oboe tilted slightly, which I think has undesirable postural consequences. If one feels tonguing on the corner of the reed is better, then the reed's position must be adjusted in a very subtle way that does not interfere with full embouchure use or overall stance.

Double Tonguing

Double tonguing, like single tonguing, must be understood in terms of tongue placement and movement. First let's look at how [k] and [g], the syllables most commonly used for the double tongue, are described.

[k] and [g]

1. The velar-palatal stop sounds [[k], [g]] share the features of breath stop and, usually, breath plosion with the [t] and [d].[23]
2. *Place of articulation:* Back of the tongue and soft palate.
3. *Typical production:* Press the raised back portion of the tongue firmly against the velum. This blocks off the air passageway, building up pressure. Lower the back of the tongue suddenly, releasing the air with a little puff or explosion. As a rule, the tongue tip remains momentarily on the floor of the mouth behind the lower front teeth.[24]

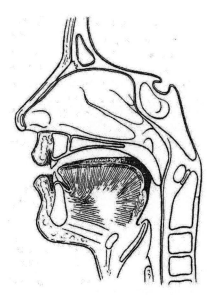

Figure 12.8. *[k] and [g]*

Double tonguing is an alternation of movement by the front of the tongue at the alveolar ridge with movement by the back of the tongue against the soft palate. However, many oboe players mis-map the [k] or [g] sound. They imagine this sound is produced in the back of the throat by the root of the tongue. When they understand the correct position the tongue should assume when making the [k], their double tonguing improves significantly.

Many teachers stress placing the [k] sound as far forward in the mouth as possible when trying to double tongue on the oboe. I believe they advocate this because either they've had personal experience mis-mapping it in the back of the throat (using the root of the tongue) or they've worked with students who have. However, when students who correctly place the [k] hear from the teacher that one should place the [k] as far forward as possible, they attempt to put it in an artificial position and experience trouble getting good results. There is no reason to place the [k] in any position other than that used in normal speech.

It is helpful to make sure to produce the [k] or [g] sound with clarity. Clarity is not achieved by changing the position, but by working with the speed of movement while maintaining air pressure.

For the [k] articulation, the back of the tongue touches the raised soft palate and then moves down. The quicker the movement, the more explosive is the release of air. One should practice the [k] articulation on its own. Experiment with this downward tongue motion. You will discover that in order for the [k] sound to match the clarity of the [t] sound, you will have to drop the back of the tongue quite quickly. This is a natural movement, working with gravity. It should be practiced on its own, with the reed alone, and with the instrument.

Having an awareness of the soft palate may improve the quality and speed of double tonguing. The soft palate should not be lowered.

The image of a seesaw is helpful. A seesaw does not change size when moving. Its weight stays the same as well. It is simply shifting position. It moves only up and down in space, not back and forth. When double tonguing, the tongue is like a seesaw: the tip of the tongue drops down, the back of the tongue moves up and then drops down from the soft palate, then the tip goes up and releases down again from the tip of the reed, over and over again.

Dancing on the Ceiling

It's helpful to recognize that the crucial points of contact for the seesawing tongue are at the top of the mouth, not the bottom. As we choreograph tongue movements for double tonguing we want to clearly recognize that the tongue is dancing on the ceiling, not the floor. When playing long tones, many oboe players have a tendency to plant the tongue against the floor of the mouth in order to get a beautiful, open sound. To maintain this tone quality when single tonguing, the front of the tongue only momentarily reaches up to the roof of the mouth to articulate, but then immediately returns to the lowered position.

This method works well for single tonguing, but holding onto this same basic conception of articulation when double tonguing makes it difficult to achieve speed. For double tonguing, the roof of the mouth is the tongue's base of operation, and it floats freely in the mouth without anchoring toward the bottom.

Riding the Wind

Just like single tonguing, some of the biggest problems with double tonguing occur not because of tongue use, but due to poor use of air. We often develop the double tongue in order to play fast passagework that is marked staccato. However, I find it very helpful at first to always think of the double tongue as a legato tongue. All double tonguing exercises should be practiced while trying to connect one note to the next. This encourages good air flow.

[t]–[k] or [d]–[g]?

Is it better to use the [t]–[k] or [d]–[g] combination for double tonguing? This is a matter of personal preference. In my own learning, I found at first I could only use the [t]–[k] combination effectively, but as I started speeding things up, I began using [d]–[g], and this seemed to help. Now I'm back to thinking [t]–[k] most of the time.

Triple Tonguing

The same movements used in double tonguing are used for triple tonguing. In fact, for many people they are exactly the same thing. Instead of the [t]–[k], [t]–[k], [t]–[k] pattern of double tonguing, triple tonguing becomes [t]–[k]–[t], [k]–[t]–[k], similar to the subtle shifts one hears in some music that alternates between 3/4 and 6/8 meters. Others advocate [t]–[k]–[t], [t]–[k]–[t], and other combinations are used as well.

Summary

When we better understand the size, structure, and function of the tongue, we can describe articulation more clearly in terms of the tongue's position, shape, and movement. We saw in chapter 6 that we improve finger technique by becoming more precise about the quality of movements the fingers make: At what angle do they approach the keys? How far do they move away from the keys? How quickly do they return? Are they moving freely or with tension?

Even though we can't see the tongue as clearly as the fingers, with our kinesthesia we can learn to monitor its movements in exactly the same way: What is the tongue's position in the oral cavity? in relation to the reed? How does the speed and quality of its movement affect the sound? Experimenting with movement is fun and takes the mystery out of articulation.

Agenda Helper 6

Tongue

Mark the statements that are true for you. Work on the ones that aren't checked.

- ❏ I have a free tongue, able to move wherever I like.
- ❏ I articulate clearly and without strain.
- ❏ I open my jaw with ease.
- ❏ I close my jaw with ease.
- ❏ I have a kinesthetic awareness of the tongue's position in my mouth as I play.
- ❏ I perceive the tip of my tongue moving up and down in relation to the reed, not back and forth.
- ❏ My use of air to produce a great sound never feels compromised by movements of the tongue.
- ❏ I actively listen for how my tongue's position affects the quality of the tone as I play.
- ❏ I actively monitor how the tongue's movements away from the reed affect tone quality.
- ❏ I have accurately mapped the root of the tongue in the throat.
- ❏ My throat is free as I articulate.
- ❏ My neck is free as I articulate.

Chapter **13**

Vibrato

Vibrato can be compared to great movie music. It enhances the performance without being noticed. But creating this illusion is no easy task.

There is much debate about vibrato. Here are some of the issues:

1. *Use:* Is it strictly a modern phenomenon for oboists? Or was it used as early as the Baroque period?
2. *Sound:* Should it be heard as a pitch fluctuation, or a fluctuation of intensity? How fast or slow should a vibrato be?
3. *Production:* Most agree that lip vibrato isn't effective for oboe, but is producing it via the throat or diaphragm better? Is vibrato produced through tension or relaxation?

It's not within the scope of *Oboemotions* to deal with historical issues or debates about musical preferences. However, *Oboemotions* does address how an oboe player's body can be best used to produce musical sounds. New research brings us closer to finding answers to questions about vibrato, but some things may just remain a mystery. An oboist reading this book who wants to know everything about the body may be hoping to find definitive answers to questions about vibrato. At this point, though, the research is ongoing and still inconclusive.

There are some very interesting recent studies of double reed vibrato, which take advantage of cinefluorography or videofluorography (basically x-ray movies of the body while playing). This research supports the long-suspected idea that laryngeal movement may be involved in producing vibrato. The vocal folds in the larynx open and close slightly. This causes fluctuations in air pressure, thus creating pulsations in the sound.

Does this mean that throat vibrato wins over diaphragm vibrato? Not exactly.

The subtle movements of the vocal folds cannot be directly sensed, so we must learn to control them in indirect ways. This is why teachers have developed exercises using felt sensations in either the abdominal or throat region which eventually give us access to the mysterious and seemingly inaccessible realm of the vibrato.

I advocate abolishing the term "diaphragm vibrato." This term is used to describe a vibrato that is initiated through pulsations of the abdominal wall. It is a means for beginners to feel that they can consciously control vibrato through an easily felt movement. Although students are often told to move the diaphragm, in reality we don't have a kinesthetic sense of the diaphragm, just as we don't have direct kinesthetic sense of vocal fold movement. The reality is that we feel the abdominal wall moving, so let's just call this an "abdominal vibrato."

Now the question arises, should we teach an abdominal vibrato? The abdominal vibrato is usually used to jumpstart vibrato for a player who is not producing it naturally. The idea is that by using abdominal movements to force the vibrato to sound for a few weeks, the vibrato will begin to emerge in a more subtle and involuntary way. When this happens, the vibrato sounds more natural and one sees and feels little or no movement in the abdominal area. In fact, at this point the vibrato is accomplished primarily in the larynx. One scientific study actually showed that most who said they were exclusively using diaphragm vibrato were really producing vibrato in the larynx.

> **The most important prescription I can provide for creating vibrato is this: listen. Listen to great singers, violinists, and cellists. Decide what makes their vibrato beautiful.**

What this proves to me is that for many oboists, this method of learning vibrato works. It may sound counterproductive to some, but *if* this method is taught without creating excess tension in the abdominal wall (and it *can* be taught in this way), then there's no reason to avoid it, because for some students, it's the only way to learn vibrato.

However, there are other ways to learn vibrato. Some practice panting at different speeds, and this helps them find a beautiful, free vibrato. Teachers who advocate throat vibrato have students whistle and then perform a variety of exercises accessing the same part of the throat engaged when whistling. Like the abdominal exercises, these start out sounding overdone, but become fluid and natural-sounding with practice.

Since studies suggest vibrato is related to laryngeal movement, you may wonder why I don't use the throat method exclusively. For one thing, some students just don't seem to be able to learn vibrato using this method. So I want to have other options available. There is an additional issue, however. If the whistling technique is taught without an awareness of the whole torso, then tone production can be adversely affected. The whole body supports vibrato with good balance and free movement of air. A possible advantage of learning abdominal vibrato is that it acknowledges the contribution of the torso. With the throat vibrato method, students pay a lot of attention to the throat. It becomes very easy to create unnecessary tension in the throat when attempting to create and sustain this whistling technique, literally choking off access to free, healthy breath support. The student must be very attentive to freeing the neck muscles while working with this technique.

Many of us have heard the "nanny goat" vibrato that results from a throat vibrato that's poorly executed. One avoids this by maintaining an awareness of free neck muscles and fully understanding how breathing works. Good balance and free breathing will assure a beautiful vibrato. If you (or your student) have trouble producing an effortless, singing vibrato, then please re-read the material on balance (chapter 3) and breathing (chapter 10).

The most important prescription I can provide for creating vibrato is this: listen. Use your imagination, remembering that the mind/body connection is a powerful one. (The importance of modeling is discussed in more detail in chapter 18). Listen to great singers, violinists, and cellists. Decide what makes their vibrato beautiful. Listen closely to how vibrato can enhance a musical phrase. Then listening, bring these high standards to your own playing.

Chapter **14**

Mapping the Oboe

To achieve the specific sound we want to make we must search for the best movement, a motion that enables us to produce the sound easily and consistently. There are many possible movement choices involving fingers, embouchure, air, and tongue. Like Goldilocks, we spend time in the practice room trying on these different choices until we find the one that feels "just right." Sometimes we find a movement that allows us to find more accuracy—better note accuracy, intonation, or timbre—and yet it still doesn't seem precisely right. Perhaps it feels or sounds strained, or is hard to achieve consistently. So even though we've made improvements, we still haven't found the perfect solution to the problem. It's difficult to pinpoint why we can't find the right movement.

Sometimes these faulty choices are made because of fundamental misconceptions about how one produces an oboe sound. This is what I describe as mis-mapping the oboe. Remember those who have mis-mapped the spine into their backs? They tend to hold themselves in a back-oriented way. This makes it impossible to find balance and puts unnecessary strain on their bodies. In the same way, someone can mis-map the ways a human body and a musical instrument interact.

The metaphor "you are your instrument" is used to imply mastery. However it is not really a useful metaphor. Making you and your instrument one, so that "you are your instrument" is *not* a goal of Body Mapping. The instrument is responsible for specific musical functions, mostly acoustical. Body Mapping helps you to accurately understand your body as a body, and then to properly map its interaction with the instrument.

This interaction of a human with an oboe is a magical blend of mind, body, and matter. Physical movement interacting with matter creates vibration. We then use a variety of means to alter the vibration's acoustical properties in order to create music that reflects an emotional state. Players who have mapped the body appropriately but mis-mapped the instrument will have trouble making appropriate movement choices.

Producing an Oboe Sound

How do we make a sound on the oboe? The most common answer I hear to this question is that we blow air into the oboe. Well, in reality, we do not blow air into the oboe. Unless a reed is inserted into the oboe you can blow air all day and no sound will be heard.

Yes, this seems obvious. But many teachers talk about blowing air into the instrument. They tell their students, "to get a better sound you must blow the air to the bell of the instrument," or "to the D key," or "to a point on the floor below the bell." So oboe players create all kinds of excess tension attempting to blow air through the instrument.

Body Mapping helps you to accurately understand your body as a body, and then to properly map its interaction with the instrument.

The reality is that oboists only need to be concerned with how to deliver air to the reed. It's the quality of the air in your mouth that makes a difference in how the oboe sounds.

It is true that some of the air you blow goes into the oboe. How else does that annoying condensation get in the octave key? But my point is that this air has nothing to do with creating beautiful music. The only sound it creates is that pesky little gurgle, signaling that a key is clogged with water!

There is air already in the oboe before you ever blow into it. There is always air in the oboe, the same atmosphere that surrounds us all the time. It is this air which carries the sound waves produced by a vibrating reed. These sound waves are altered by the bore of the instrument and by the movements of our fingers and travel through the atmosphere, reaching the ears as sound.

Myth Buster

Blow the air to _____.

Some of the ways teachers fill in the blank:

1. The D key
2. The bell
3. A spot on the floor
4. The back of the auditorium
5. Other

Any of these options can be destructive to the oboe player.

Why this myth has helped some people:

If the student isn't supporting the tone with enough air to begin with, then the suggestion to blow to a spot far away often improves the sound. The student will either increase the quantity or the speed of the air, or both. This increased air pressure improves the tone quality.

How this myth is harmful:

To create a great sound, the oboist must always carefully monitor the air at the reed. In the attempt to blow air at a point away from the reed, the musician begins to force, or overblow. This overblowing has an adverse effect on the oboe sound as well as creating unnecessary tension in the body.

This myth is often just an extension of the column of air fantasy discussed in chapter 10. The student is encouraged to imagine an artificial column in the body that extends through the instrument, even to the back of the concert hall. The attempt to realize this fantasy can create a great deal of strain in the player's body. It also takes focus away from where it's needed (at the reed), making it difficult to embody the music.

Myth Replacement

A quality sound depends on the quality of the air in the mouth. Find the right air pressure to make a beautiful sound.

Air pressure, reed vibration, and embouchure work together, creating a resonant and focused sound from the instrument (see chapters 9 and 10). Many players make the mistake of blowing harder in order to project the sound more. A well-focused, resonant sound will project at all dynamic levels.

It is helpful to experience air pressure and air flow away from the instrument. Practice breathing exercises. Blow a balloon, a candle, a piece of paper against the wall, etc. Then use the information you learned about your own breathing to help find the right amount of air for a beautiful sound. Your ear will let you know when you have it right!

Peripersonal Space

The instrument is just a pipe, a tube, a piece of plumbing. This tube amplifies the sound of a vibrating reed, but its conical bore also contributes to the instrument's unique timbre. The holes along the pipe are covered with keys. Our fingers move on these keys and alter the pitch. Pads underneath the keys are placed with precision, or else leaks will disrupt the sound. Likewise the fingers must move efficiently so that they are placed in a precise manner on the keys without disrupting the musical line.

Although the phrase "you are your instrument" can be misleading, recent discoveries by neuroscientists are helping us understand ways we do "become one with" the instrument. Scientists are exploring peripersonal space, the area immediately surrounding the body. The brain treats this area differently than space farther away from the body. Researchers are finding out that the brain maps this area as if it were part of the body.

Have you every noticed how much information you get about your food through the fork with which you're eating? The fork acts as an extension of your hand, and even though it is a completely inanimate object, it provides accurate information to your brain about the size, texture, and density of the food. Your perceptual experience of the food is not located at your fingertips but rather, is felt at the tip of this inanimate object. It's as if your fingertips extend to the end of the fork. This is possible because of complex neuronal connections that help the brain map peripersonal space.

Certainly reed-makers appreciate the brain's ability to extend one's perception of space while using tools. We gather a great deal of information about our reeds through the knife we use to scrape the cane.

As scientists continue to uncover the ways brains map peripersonal space, there are likely to be fantastic applications for musicians, particularly related to teaching and practicing. In the meantime, musicians who recognize the intimate way that their brain maps peripersonal space will want to make certain it is being mapped adequately and accurately. What is the actual circumference of the instrument? I don't mean you should measure this, but some people switch from clarinet or flute to playing the oboe and haven't sufficiently registered the difference in circumference. Likewise, the length of the instrument, its weight, the distance from one key to another—all these things must be accurately mapped in order to achieve accurate performance.

Finding Your Voice

Oboemotions demonstrates what a marvelously complex feat playing the oboe is. It combines a multitude of subtle mental and physical processes. Properly mapping the oboe simplifies this feat for the performer.

The two blades of a double reed are sometimes compared to the vocal cords. Singers know that the movement of air causes the vocal cords to vibrate, and the amount of air pressure on the cords can dramatically alter the timbre. Adjustments of the vocal cords create color and pitch variation. Oboists make adjustments to the reed with the embouchure and tongue to create dynamics and color variations.

Singers monitor the vocal cords mainly with the brain. Through practice they learn to think a pitch or timbre, and it happens. Oboists can approach playing in the same way. With practice you develop the ability to imagine and then instantly produce a sound. When playing, notice that your embouchure, tongue, and air are manipulating two blades of cane that act as the instrument's vocal cords.

Then you really are singing.

Body Mapping Practice 5

Mapping the Oboe

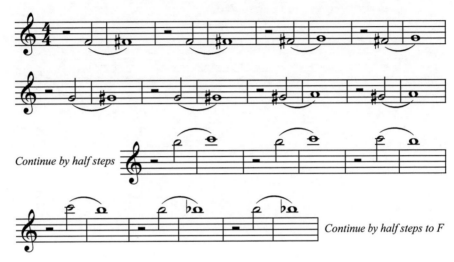

Figure 14.1. *Half-step warm-up*

1. Use this warm-up as an opportunity to remap your relationship with the oboe.
2. Notice yourself first, and find good balance.
3. Notice the way the reed tickles your lips when it vibrates.
4. As you play this warm-up, think of using appropriate effort at the reed.
5. Are you using excess effort, trying to create a column of air that reaches the bell of the instrument, or beyond?
6. Or is your focus on creating appropriate air pressure at the reed, so that it vibrates with full resonance in all registers?
7. Experiment with how air pressure affects air flow.
8. Take time to notice the differences in the way the reed vibrates in the low register of the oboe compared to the high register.
9. Notice how your body responds to these differences.

This lilting solo from Stravinsky's *Pulcinella* (figure 14.2) is a wonderful test for how well you are mapping the oboe.

1. Pay attention to how air affects the reed vibration while maintaining a free neck and good overall balance.
2. What combination of air, embouchure, and tongue position does the reed need to play a beautiful-sounding C (in the middle of the staff)? high C? low C?
3. What embouchure adjustments are really necessary through the course of this solo?

4. Does the position of the reed in the mouth need to shift?
5. When, and how much?

Figure 14.2. *Igor Stravinsky,* Pulcinella *siciliano*

Once you've worked out these issues, play this solo in its entirety. Bring out the emotions of grace and elegance associated with a siciliano while always monitoring for balance and ease.

Chapter 15

Reed-making

What materials do we use to make reeds? Cane, knives, plaques, mandrels, cutting blocks, thread, shapers, gouging machines—I'm sure there are other things you can add to the list. Just don't forget the most important material needed to make a reed. That's the reed-maker—you!

Unfortunately, many who make reeds are so concerned with the process of reed-making that they completely forget about themselves. They sit or stand, hunched over this tiny piece of cane, for hours sometimes, hardly noticing how tense their body is, and how poorly they are breathing, until after they're done. Then they wonder why their neck feels strained or their back is sore.

So I urge you to take the knowledge about the body that you've gained in *Oboemotions* and apply it to yourself as you gouge cane, sharpen a knife, or scrape the tip just a little bit thinner.

Setup

Don't be haphazard about where you make reeds. Recognize that this is an activity that takes a lot of your time on a regular basis and prepare a space for reed-making that is truly comfortable. The lighting should be good. The desk or table you use should be at an appropriate height for either sitting or standing, whichever you prefer. If you sit, use a chair that is comfortable and the right size for your body as well as for the desk.

Warm-up

Before you begin, take a little time to notice yourself. You are the reed-maker. The better shape you're in, the better chance you have that the work you do will be successful.

Often you're in a rush, barely finding time to work on reeds at all. But it really just takes one minute to notice yourself. How are you sitting? Can you find better balance? How free are your neck muscles? What is your breathing like?

> Recognize that reed-making is an activity that takes a lot of your time on a regular basis and prepare a space for it that is truly comfortable.

You may even want to do a couple of stretches. Reed-making is a physical activity, and gentle stretches of the hands and forearms as well as shoulder and head rolls are all excellent warm-ups.

Just as it's very common for oboe players to bring the head forward and down when playing, it's just as prevalent for reed-makers to collapse the chest and drop the head down as they become more and more involved in the reed-making process. Maintain an inclusive awareness when you make reeds to avoid this habit. You may find it helpful to take breaks at regular intervals (perhaps every fifteen minutes) just to spend a minute to find balance over the chair or floor, and then resume the work at hand.

Stay Sharp!

A sharp knife is crucial for making a good reed. It also makes for less strain on your body. Ever notice how you use your arms when the knife is sharp, and how that use changes as the knife dulls? Working with a sharp knife feels effortless. A dull knife forces you to exert more pressure with hands and forearms. This often results in tension felt in the whole body.

If you have a sharp knife, you must make it a priority to maintain the knife's edge as you work on a reed. You may have to sharpen the blade several times even when just making one reed. The extra effort is well worth it—for the reed, and for you!

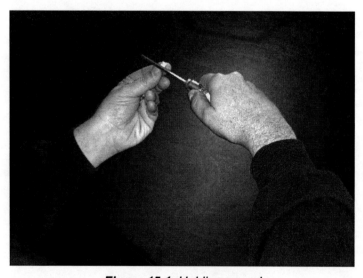

***Figure 15.1.** Holding a reed*

Finding a comfortable way to hold the reed and knife will give you the freedom to scrape a reed in any direction.

Technique

Some oboe players have suffered injuries to hands or arms, not from playing the instrument, but from reed-making. Understanding the arm's structure and how the parts of the arm function will help reed-makers avoid these overuse injuries. Double reed players should develop reed-making techniques that maintain proper relationships between hands, wrists, and forearms. This includes techniques for holding a reed while scraping, binding cane to the staple, holding and sharpening a knife, and for shaping and gouging cane.

Figures 15.2a–b. Sharpening a knife

15.2a. *With ulnar deviation*

Consistently gripping the knife in a thumb-oriented manner may result in pain or injury.

15.2b. *Without ulnar deviation*

Adjust the angle of the knife to the sharpening stone for more effective use of the arms.

Reed Yoga

Reed-making can take a lot of time. Some reed-makers spend all that time locked in one position. It is better for the reed-maker's health to become comfortable with a variety of positions. Figures 15.3–7 show various positions from which you can make good reeds. Have fun exploring "reed yoga," finding your own favorite poses for making great reeds while maintaining a healthy body.

Figure 15.3. "Reed Yoga"

Have fun exploring "reed yoga," finding your own favorite poses for making great reeds while maintaining a healthy body.

Figure 15.4. Stressful reed-making

Reed-makers often collapse the chest and drop the head down as they concentrate more and more on the reed but neglect the body.

Figure 15.5. The curl

The head leads a sequential forward curl of the vertebrae in order to bring you closer to a light or table without straining the neck or compressing the chest.

Figure 15.6. *Using the table for arm support*

Resting the forearm on a table or reed desk provides great stability for scraping a reed and allows the body to stay relaxed.

Figure 15.7. *The dugout position*

With elbows resting near the knees, arms feel supported while the lower back lengthens comfortably.

Chapter 16

Making a Case

Q: How does an oboe get to a gig?

A: In its case.

Oboe and English horn cases come in many shapes and sizes. Sometimes these cases get put into larger cases in order to accommodate other things: music, reed equipment, tuners, and metronomes. These larger cases might be backpacks or briefcases, computer bags or small suitcases with wheels.

Take time to think about how you carry your stuff. Often we carry equipment every day, even several times a day. Over time, the way we carry things can take a toll on our bodies. Those who have hand, back, or neck pain from playing the oboe sometimes aggravate the pain because of the way they carry their case.

There have been many innovative designs for cases over the past few years. Now one can find lightweight oboe and English horn cases as well as double cases styled like backpacks. Many have two straps so the weight of the case can be evenly distributed over the back and arm structure. From an ergonomic point of view, these are the best cases available.

Many cases are designed for holding in your hand. If you have one of these, then on a regular basis you should alternate the hand with which you carry it. If the case feels heavy, you should use a shoulder strap. If it

> **Over time, the way we carry things can take a toll on our bodies.**

feels heavy but doesn't have a shoulder strap, then have one made for it.

With good alignment, our bodies are able to bear a reasonable amount of extra weight with ease. However, any weight will have the tendency to drag the body down if we are not conscious of our alignment. So take time to notice how you pick your case up and bring it to you.

1. As you pick up your oboe case, is your neck tense or free? Are you moving from your waist, or do you hinge at your hip joints?
2. As you carry the case, do you allow the weight of the case to pull you back toward your heels? Or do you feel its weight being delivered through the central arches of your feet?
3. Once you arrive at a gig, you take the instrument out of its case and put it together. How do you do this? Take the time to notice.

Earlier in this book you read about how important sitting and standing are for good oboe playing. Prior to a rehearsal or a performance, you can begin warming up before you ever play a note, even before you put the instrument together. By noticing how you are sitting or standing you are warming up your kinesthetic awareness in preparation for playing the instrument. Open the case and put the instrument together with care. Notice your alignment and breathing, as well as the emotions you bring with you. This sort of inclusive awareness should prepare you for whatever the rehearsal or performance may bring.

Chapter 17
Performance Anxiety

Performance anxiety is a normal part of our musical culture. Many of our greatest classical performers admit they experience varying degrees of nervousness when performing. My favorite anecdote about performance anxiety relates to Caruso, regarded as the greatest opera singer of his time. When an acquaintance asked him, "How can you be nervous? You are the great Caruso—you have given hundreds of fantastic performances!" Caruso retorted, "Yes, but every time I perform, people expect me to sound like Caruso!"

Classical tradition has created a musical culture that puts a lot of pressure on performers. Musicians dress formally and are spotlighted on a stage, separated from their audience. The easy availability of recordings has added to this pressure, raising both performers' and audiences' expectations of perfection. Not all cultures operate in this manner. There are societies where music making is a communal activity. Everyone participates, either singing or playing an instrument for ritual or celebratory purposes. People raised in these cultures rarely suffer from performance anxiety—many don't even know what it is.

Excellent books and articles have been written to help musicians develop strategies for coping with or overcoming performance anxiety. If you have a consistent problem performing because of uncontrollable shaking, severe stomach problems, sweaty hands, dry mouth, and the like, then you should seek the help offered by these books, or a teacher, counselor, or other specialist.

Some performers use beta-blockers—drugs that quiet your sympathetic nervous system—to alleviate stage fright. I find it interesting that one's mind can be quieted using beta-blockers, a drug initially designed to engender a physical response in the body. Beta-blockers seem to be further proof of a strong mind/body connection.

When musical training ignores the body, it becomes much easier for performance anxiety to manifest itself in physical ways. Body Mapping was developed as a response to the tremendous misinformation about the human body on which much classical music training has been based. Body Mapping can powerfully reduce the symptoms of performance anxiety because it trains the performer to develop an awareness of how the body contributes to good performance and then encourages the performer to increase that awareness every day in the practice room.

One of the surest ways to deal with nervousness is to get out of your head by focusing on tactile sensation. Notice small things like the temperature in the room, the way your clothes feel, the pressure of fingers against the keys, or the amount of resistance in the reed. If you tend to be short of breath when you are nervous, it's much more powerful to rely on the sensations of rib movement (how are the ribs moving on inhalation? on exhalation?) than just thinking, "I should breathe from the diaphragm" (an essentially meaningless phrase). If you've trained yourself every day in the practice room to notice the ribs in relation to breath and phrasing, then it becomes very comfortable to work with this in a performance situation.

> When musical training ignores the body, it becomes much easier for performance anxiety to manifest itself in physical ways.

Shallow breathing is a normal reaction to performance anxiety. If this happens to you, first notice the ribs, then observe the reaction of the abdominal wall and the pelvic floor to rib movement. Are you holding the abdominal muscles in a way that prevents free breathing? Is posture inhibiting the reflexive actions of the pelvic diaphragm? Again, because these are things you've experimented with and maintained an awareness of every single time you've practiced, it becomes relatively easy to access them anytime—even when you are very nervous.

Body Mapping encourages practicing based on understanding the true structure of the human body and acknowledging that quality movement creates better music. This sort of practice results in a different type of performance than one based on traditional rote practice.

Performance anxiety is not something to think about *after* the performance. It is something we must deal with long before the performance. We deal with it in the practice room daily. If your nervousness takes the form of shaking hands, then you should spend time in the practice room improving awareness of your hands and how you use them. You improve your awareness by studying anatomy, videotaping yourself or using a mirror, and answering questions like the following:

1. How much pressure do your fingers exert on the keys?
2. Could they exert less pressure?
3. How far away from the keys do the fingers move?
4. Could they move less?
5. At what angle do you hold your hands in relation to the keys?
6. What are you doing with your thumbs during technical passagework?
7. How are you using your wrists to support the work of the fingers?
8. How does the arm's structure support finger movement?

These are just some of the issues you should be exploring with your teacher and on your own in the practice room. (For more ideas, see chapter 6). During a performance, instead of your mind becoming overwhelmed by the thought that your hands are shaking uncontrollably you can begin to notice these many specific physical elements related to playing the oboe that you've already explored in the practice room. You will discover that your mind can make room for these other thoughts and you will begin performing better.

Chapter 18
Practicing Oboemotions

Effective Practice

Practicing is discovery. But what do we want to discover? In other words, what's the point of practice?

Right now, I think the point of practice is discovering how to make beautiful playing easier.

But for years my goal was discovering how to manage the difficult work of beautiful playing.

Maybe this was because I knew, at least subconsciously, that the oboe was supposed to be difficult. So I managed to find ways to improve accuracy and to get through a performance situation without embarrassment. In fact things sounded pretty good, but felt difficult. A performance felt more like a trial—me against the oboe.

Now my goal is to make great music in the easiest way possible. I spend time in the practice room figuring out ways to make the music sound good and feel easy. I'm much more satisfied with my performances now that I've engaged this new method of practicing. A performance feels more like a party now—a celebration of the music. Playing the oboe is more playful.

Emotion

Oboists are often drawn to the instrument for its ability to evoke strong feelings in listeners. Merely the timbre of the instrument is often perceived as emotionally charged—rich and poignant, or in the case of the English horn, melancholy.

Great composers have tapped into this emotional richness, writing melodies for the instrument as diverse as Bach's *Ich Habe Genug*, Ravel's *Tombeau de Couperin*, Brahms's *Violin Concerto*, and many more.

Our bodies react to emotion. We stiffen with fear, flush with anger, shake when nervous. Even our breathing constantly changes in response to feelings. It quickens, slows, or momentarily stops altogether. Listening to emotional music can invoke these same bodily responses.

> My goal is to make great music in the easiest way possible.

Some of these normal physical reactions to emotion, however, can interfere with a musician's ability to make music well. Bodies must be poised and buoyant; embouchures, flexible; and arms and fingers, relaxed.

So how can we be open to the emotions of music and yet maintain the mechanical advantage our bodies need to perform well? One can have the best of both worlds by expanding musical awareness to always include somatic awareness. In fact, the grounding gained through Body Mapping, Alexander Technique, or other somatic disciplines allows one to open up more fully to emotion and give one the ability to instantly transform those feelings into music.

Setting the Right Conditions

How does one incorporate new methods into daily practice? The process of integrating the discoveries made through Body Mapping may be different than the sort of practice you are used to. You may be comfortable with the type of practice used for learning a new skill, such as a new fingering for a note. This practice involves rote repetition until the skill becomes second nature. However, Body Mapping often involves *un*learning a habit that may have developed over years or even decades. This undoing requires patience, persistence, and the development of certain practice skills that you may not have used before.

Within the first year of learning to play an oboe, one immediately begins to develop habits. A habit is an action that through repetition becomes part of your subconscious. We each develop very personal habits for blowing, articulation, and fingering patterns. And it's a good thing our brains have the ability to do this; otherwise we'd be overwhelmed with trying to remember the basics (how do I finger that note? where does my tongue touch the reed? etc.) and we'd be unable to make a phrase sing. Over time we become so conditioned to doing things in our particular manner that we're no longer really even conscious of what we are doing.

However, in order to correct a Body Mapping problem, it is important that we have the ability to analyze the process we use for playing a phrase—both conscious and subconscious. In fact, we must raise the subconscious to the conscious level if we are going to make improvements in our playing. Developing kinesthetic awareness is the key to unlocking these processes. Kinesthetic awareness allows us to become actively engaged in every moment of music making, giving us the ability to allow a good habit to take over and also the chance to stop a habit that's getting in the way of making great music.

In chapter 1 I stated:

Finding good oboemotions requires the following approach to practicing:

1. Find the emotion (mind)
2. Find the motions that best bring out the emotion (body)
3. Repeat these motions, with emotion (mind/body)

Now it's time to look at each of these a bit more carefully. But first it's important to underscore another point made in chapter 1. The work of Body Mapping is done in the practice room. When successful, it brings about changes so profound that the quality of your performances may improve dramatically. During a performance you are concerned with musical matters, with communicating a good story to your audience through music. You will not be thinking about anatomical issues anymore. Because of the way you've practiced, you will have conditioned yourself to naturally associate good musical sounds with good body use. You will only need to shift your focus to physical matters if you hear problems—missed notes, poor intonation, weak tone quality, etc.—which prevent you from telling that musical story in the way you intended.

Step 1: Find the Emotion (Mind)

Discovering the most appropriate intention for a musical score is a multilayered process. It involves understanding music at two levels:

1. What is the specific musical style of the piece of music in front of me?
2. What is the more general emotional mood conveyed by this music?

These decisions are not always clear-cut. They involve not just listening to your own emotional response to the music, but learning about the composer and the historical context, studying the score carefully, examining descriptive words, metronome markings, harmonic shifts, accents, dynamics, etc. All of these are clues to understanding a composer's intentions. Of course you also want to be certain the edition of music you are using is faithful to the composer's intentions and makes clear what markings are the composer's and which are editorial. It's also helpful to listen to other performances, both on recordings and in live performance.

Once an overall style and emotion is decided, you work on playing each phrase and understanding how it relates to the whole. You should always acknowledge the emotion you feel as you hear or play a phrase, then evaluate if this emotion is validated by the various stylistic and compositional issues already explored when studying the piece as a whole.

The emotion the music inspires may not be one with which you are personally familiar. You learn the emotion, with all its nuances, as you play the music. One of the great benefits of being a musician is gaining a tremendous range of emotional experience that one may not have otherwise experienced. Of course the price for this is being emotionally available to the music so that these emotions are fully experienced and assimilated.

Once you are confident that you have found the appropriate emotion, go to step 2.

Step 2: Find the Motions That Best Bring Out the Emotion (Body)

This is sometimes a simple process. Often the proper movements are found immediately, based on past work playing other music (including scales and warm-up routines). Other times it is quite difficult to find the right movement. It requires a lot of trial and error, recording or videotaping yourself, or perhaps getting the help of another person. You want to be certain that you are using the most efficient movements necessary to create precisely the right sound for the musical phrase. This is where Body Mapping is so useful.

Sometimes discoveries made about the body map can be incorporated into one's playing immediately. But often these discoveries involve undoing long-held habits. This requires patience and persistence and can sometimes take a long time to correct. But the effort is always worthwhile.

How do you unlearn a habit and replace it with a new, more productive habit? First you clearly identify the new goal and understand the value of achieving it. Imagine you have just read the section in chapter 6 about the arms and realize for the first time that you play the oboe with ulnar deviation. You recognize that this has been limiting your ability to play certain passagework and understand the many other reasons you should start using your hands in a different manner. But how should you practice?

The trick is not to become obsessed with the goal. Instead, make the goal useful by taking the time to explore the path to the goal.

Set a reasonable goal for yourself. Avoid a negative goal, such as "I will no longer play with ulnar deviation." You want to positively reinforce a new habit based on increasing your awareness. A positive and attainable goal might be: "I will play the oboe with increased awareness, noticing the alignment of my pinky fingers with my elbows."

The trick is not to become obsessed with this goal. Instead, make the goal useful by taking the time to explore the path to the goal. Constantly thinking about holding the hand in a particular position will often lead to a different kind of tension; a posture. It will be more useful to begin expanding your awareness of the hand in relation to the arm.

1. Carefully study drawings of the whole arm.
2. Then notice your own pinky fingers and their relationship to your arms.
3. Notice your wrists.
4. Develop an awareness of a whole arm and the arm's relationship to the spine and overall body alignment.
5. Then maintain this awareness as you bring the arm to the oboe.
6. Notice how much easier breathing and maintaining balance are as you easily bring a whole arm to the oboe—an arm that aligns the pinky to the elbow, and an arm that is kinesthetically connected to the rest of the body.

Now that you've brought a whole arm to the oboe, you should begin to notice the quality of movement that your fingers have on the keys of the instrument.

1. Are the fingers tense or relaxed?
2. On a scale of 1 to 10, with 1 relaxed and 10 tense, where do your fingers rate?
3. If they are a 6, how do they feel with more tension? Maybe an 8?
4. How would they feel with less tension—perhaps a 4?
5. How do the fingers approach the keys?

6. Are they on a horizontal plane with the keys or do they approach the keys at an angle?
7. How much of an angle?
8. Would the fingers feel more relaxed if they approached the keys in a different way?

With this sort of improved kinesthetic awareness of the arms and fingers you will eventually find that you are no longer playing with ulnar deviation. Your goal has been achieved, yet you didn't really focus on the goal. Instead you found the conditions by which the goal could be achieved.

The Alexander Technique describes the goal-oriented form of practicing as *end-gaining*. Often end-gaining just provokes a different sort of tension. In place of end-gaining, the Alexander Technique advocates using inclusive awareness to create the *means-whereby* a goal can be achieved.

Mapping Performance Space

One must be certain to use the same movements when practicing that one will need when performing. Good performers learn to claim the performance space necessary to project music's emotions to an audience whether they are playing in a cramped practice room at a music conservatory or on the stage of a large concert hall. This is not pretending (i.e., "even though I'm playing in a cramped practice room, I will imagine I'm in Carnegie Hall."). It is realistically assessing the movements needed to make great music. Oboists' movements tend to be limited when their playing is confined to the space between themselves and the oboe bell. When performers command a larger space for performance, their playing is different, more expressive. Music becomes communication.

Step 3: Repetition (Mind/Body)

Now, let's explore the third part of practicing: *Repeat these motions, with emotion.*

Once one determines the appropriate emotions and figures out the proper motions to bring them out, then practicing becomes a process of repeating the chosen movements with full-on emotional intention. Consistent repetition will bring successful results. There are a few things to watch out for at this stage, however.

Mindless Repetition

Mindless repetition is boring. Find creative ways to pay attention while you practice. "Paying" attention is an interesting figure of speech. Kay Hooper, an Alexander Technique Teacher and author of *Sensory Tune-ups*, brings out a coin purse to help her students understand attention. How much attention are you giving during practice—twenty-five cents worth? one hundred dollars worth? Attention, unlike money, is something we have an unlimited supply of, so don't be a miser!

Intention

You've heard the expression, "Once more...with feeling!" Essentially this is another way of expressing the third rule of practicing. One should avoid falling into the trap of repeating only the movements without the emotion or vice versa. Some people feel they should reserve the emotion for the performance. Just like attention, there's also no limit to the amount of emotion we can draw on. Think of a great Broadway actress who must give a powerfully emotional performance that an audience finds believable. She may perform many times a week, sometimes for months or years. She finds a way to bring out the emotion consistently every time it's needed. She also learns not to be overtaken by the emotion, leaving the character behind when she's not performing.

Self-talk

We all experience self-talk while practicing, the little voices in your mind that want to intrude on the musical flow. Some people carry on such involved conversations in their head while they're playing that they hardly notice the sound coming out of the horn.

Negative self-talk can be especially debilitating—"I sound lousy"; "I'll never sound as good as Heinz Holliger"; "Maybe I should just wait tables for a living"; and so forth. Recognize that these voices in your head represent something: the voice of a parent or teacher, or a colleague's thoughtless remark. Away from the oboe, it's helpful to sort out just who these voices are, and how you allow them to still haunt you. You may decide you need to work out unresolved issues, to understand how they still impede you. How did you learn this negative self-talk? None of us is born with self-criticism; we learn it.

When practicing and performing, these voices can distract you from hearing the music you are playing. Notice the voices, then let them go as you return to the music making at hand.

Open your ears to the nonverbal cues you are receiving—the sounds emanating from the instrument, the feel of the tongue on the reed, the muscles of the face, the movement of the jaw, the gathering and lengthening spine, your emotions—and respond to these things. If a note is sharp, fix it; if the vibrato seems too slow, speed it up; if the reed is slipping too far into the mouth, then pull it out; if you're running out of breath, take in more air; etc. Continue intending the music, listening objectively to how it's being projected and making adjustments when necessary. That's plenty to do without giving power to a running verbal commentary in your mind as well. Yes, words will pop up. Just allow them to be there. By exploring ways not to succumb to the need to answer them, over time they will lose their impact.

After playing a passage, you can use constructive self-talk to evaluate what you just did. "Was that a successful performance? What was particularly good? What needs improvement? How can I improve on it? What if I tried playing it in some other manner?" You will find that by lessening (or eliminating) the dialogue while performing you will be able to react much more effectively to the other important sensory stimuli you are receiving. And you will perform better.

Honest Evaluation

Being able to listen objectively to one's own playing is an important practice skill that's difficult to master. For many of us it is just as much of a challenge to have an accurate impression of how we use our body when we perform. And this is an equally important practice skill.

Fortunately there are many ways to work on improving both of these skills. Having a trusting friend or teacher is vital, but there is much you can do on your own. Practicing in front of a mirror (or with several mirrors) can be very useful. Today there are a multitude of ways to make audio and video recordings. Take advantage of these tools and learn to be your own best critic.

In addition, make time to evaluate what you really like about other performers. The value of modeling should never be underestimated. Our brains have "mirror neurons" that respond to the actions we observe in others. In other words, just listening carefully to someone else performing activates some of the same circuitry in our brains that we would use if we were actually playing the oboe ourselves. Beyond this, the mirror neurons act as body maps that simulate what another person's body maps are doing. So paying close attention to another performer is a form of mental practice in which you can actually begin to take on some of the attributes of the admired performer. This is why students so often seem to take on habits (postural or otherwise) of their teachers, even habits that the teacher has never explicitly discussed with the student.

Practicing without the Oboe

Throughout *Oboemotions* I've proposed that oboe playing improves with greater awareness of the body. Just as it's important to study musical scores and listen to great performers, and it's also helpful to get regular exercise, and/or to practice disciplines such as tai chi, yoga, or Pilates. These disciplines increase awareness of your body and its movements. Breathing exercises are invaluable. Practice them standing up, sitting, lying down, or draped over a physio-ball.

Practice on the reed alone. Hold the reed against the embouchure as if the instrument was attached to it. Play a pitch on the reed with a well-focused and ringing tone (the note C works well for an American-scrape reed). Practice how you start and finish a note; practice making crescendos and diminuendos without altering the pitch; experiment with various articulations—all using the reed alone. This is a great way to analyze the most efficient means of blowing and articulating. It's also a wonderful way to maintain practice while suffering from certain injuries, especially hand and arm problems.

It's easy to accumulate muscular tension throughout a day, perhaps due to emotional stress, or hard work, or just driving through heavy traffic. So it's important to have a regular way of relieving these built-up muscular tensions. Alexander Technique teaches "lying down work," or "structured rest"—a very effective way of releasing tension (see the appendix for Barbara Conable's description of structured rest). Certain types of meditation can also be helpful. Some may need the guidance of competent, professional massage therapists or chiropractors.

Attitude

I've stated the third rule of practicing in a way that's pithy and easy to remember: *repeat these motions with emotion.* But the previous sections show that this wording isn't completely adequate. Perhaps a more accurate way of explaining this stage of practice is to say: *consistently and creatively repeat the movement with an inclusive awareness until it becomes reliable.* This statement acknowledges the mind/body relationship of emotion that one discovers through inclusive awareness and also stresses that practice is a personal and creative endeavor. But a person's attitude greatly influences both the ability to maintain awareness and be creative.

Practicing can be a grind. In order to train muscles and brain, and thus create new habits, repetition is an essential element of practice. Many people are bored easily by repetition. So it helps to create some variety within repetition: keep the notes the same but change dynamics, or add accents, change the tempo, rhythms, etc.

Often we feel a psychological pressure when practicing. We have a limited amount of time to learn something, or we impose pressure by constantly comparing ourselves to others in a negative way. These things also make practicing a grind.

When one wants to make progress, then practice is serious business. Practice is a discipline which must be pursued every day. And although practice is serious business, the best practice is conducted with joy. So make it your mission to discover the joy of practicing. There are many paths to joy. Some have found it through religion, therapy, meditation, or just having a sense of humor. But a body in a joyful state reacts differently than a body in a depressed, grave, or anxious state.

Of course you won't always be ecstatic playing music. Some days we come to the instrument depressed, angry, tired, or with a variety of other emotions. It's important to notice what emotions you bring to the instrument and how those emotions may influence the ways you move. Through Body Mapping you will still know how to move well in order to make great music no matter what emotions life may be dealing you.

Make it your mission to discover the joy of practicing.

When Alexander taught the "whispered AH," which he considered a key element for developing good "use," he asked students to think of something amusing. He recognized that this put the muscles of the face and the whole body in a state of readiness. Perhaps you've noticed certain superstar performers such as Yo Yo Ma, James Galway, and Luciano Pavarotti who seem to always have a twinkle in their eyes and who smile so readily when they finish a performance. A well-regarded oboist once described a good oboe tone as "always having a smile in it."

There have been many investigations proving that our physical state affects our mental state. A recent study gave a group of people Botox injections in their forehead. With the injections they couldn't furrow their brows anymore. They suffered fewer bouts of depression than a control group without the injections who still had the ability to furrow the brow. How many oboe players have you seen with furrowed brows? I used to see one when I looked in the mirror.

The awareness one gains through Body Mapping allows one to more easily access joy.

One maintains an awareness of the body while playing and monitors good alignment to support expressive tone production. An aligned body expresses confidence to an audience and makes the performer feel better as well.

Don't we play music because we love it? Allow the oboe tone and your body to express the love you feel for the music. If you've become out of touch with the love that initially drew you to playing music, then it's time to find that spark again. It *is* a feat to play the oboe. But despite the dramas of reed-making, competitions, and job hunting, allow the oboe to help you find joy in your life and your music. Practicing the oboe can always be your refuge.

Put the "Play" Back into Playing Your Instrument

Nobody really can define what music is, but it is certainly a very powerful force. Music can have a profound effect on emotions. Therapists use music in powerful ways to impact the psyche. With Body Mapping, one discovers that the musical instrument can also be a powerful tool for monitoring one's physical health. The best sounds are produced by a well-used body. We learn to associate a certain type of sound with good playing techniques. When we hear that the sound is off (out of tune, strained, weak, etc.) we find physical balance so that we can recover the great sound we want to hear.

Through Body Mapping we develop good oboemotions and discover what ease of movement means in relation to the instrument: how fingers can move fluidly to create a wonderful cadenza, or how the tongue can move effortlessly to create a quick staccato, to cite just two examples. When the fingers aren't fluid, we must find balance. Perhaps a wrist is overextended or the shoulder joint is being held too far back. When the tongue isn't effortless, then we find balance. How is the skull balanced over the A-O joint? Are the muscles behind the chin tight? This constant monitoring of how the body supports beautiful music making, when pursued on a daily basis in practice and performance, begins to have a profound and positive effect on the general state of our physical health.

Instead of the oboe being known as "the ill wind that nobody blows good," thanks to Body Mapping, oboe players can blow good wind that doesn't make anybody ill!

Happy Ending

So there you have it. Oboemotions are a celebration of the oboe—this instrument with the hauntingly beautiful and expressive sound. An instrument which can sing the joy of Rossini, the anguish of Aida, which can dance with Salome, and remind us of frantic ducks or floating swans. Oboemotions are a celebration of day-to-day living—a celebration of this habit we're addicted to.

We constantly feed our oboe addiction, spending hours of time playing it, taking care of it, traveling on its behalf, spending money on it, and yes, even making reeds for it. This instrument, this positive addiction, turns out to be a glorious thing. It's capable of transforming our daily lives both emotionally and physically.

Celebrate the emotions. Celebrate the motions.

Body Mapping Practice **6**

Practice

Improvisation is a wonderful way to connect with your emotions and kinesthesia. Many oboe players feel uncomfortable improvising because they are not encouraged to try it. It is now associated more with jazz than classical training, despite the fact that improvisation used to be an important part of the classical tradition. If you are not used to improvising, start with something simple: improvising on one note. Pick your favorite note and vary its length, color, dynamic. Can your chosen note express anger? peace? fear? Have fun being expressive and creative with just one note. Then choose a favorite scale or mode and improvise using only these notes. Or you can improvise freely, with no predetermined limits. Imitate a bird, frog, or police siren! Or just close your eyes and play a melody you love by ear.

Agenda Helper 7
Practicing Oboemotions

Mark the statements that are true for you. Work on the ones that aren't checked.

- ❏ I clearly perceive my emotions when I practice.
- ❏ I clearly perceive my motions when I practice.
- ❏ My body map is accurate.
- ❏ My body map is adequate.
- ❏ I perceive my position clearly as I play.
- ❏ I am self-perceiving and world-perceiving as I practice.
- ❏ I know that muscles respond to intention.
- ❏ I take periodic rests during my practice sessions.
- ❏ When I play, I am attentive to how I am doing as well as to what I am doing.
- ❏ I intend what I do, and I intend how I do it.
- ❏ I intend to play with freedom, awareness, and fluidity, and I carry out my intention.
- ❏ If I can conceive it, I can do it.

Appendix

Coaching Constructive Rest

by Barbara Conable

Many students of the Alexander Technique practice "constructive rest," also called "structured rest" or "lying down." Given below is how Barbara Conable coaches constructive rest, incorporating the principles of Body Mapping.

When constructive rest is practiced regularly (daily for about fifteen minutes) it significantly improves body awareness and helps the body unlearn long-held habits. Many Alexander Technique books include descriptions of how to get in a good resting position, and certainly the guidance of a teacher is invaluable. Constructive rest is best carried out supine on a floor (carpeted, on a blanket, or a yoga mat), with knees bent and feet on the floor. Hands should rest gently on the floor, or can be comfortably folded on the chest or abdomen. In order to release tension in the neck muscles, it may be necessary to place a book or pile of books under the head (anywhere from two to six inches may be needed).

I thank Barbara Conable for allowing me to include her description of constructive rest that follows. I have found it invaluable for my own progress.

—Stephen Caplan

Day 1

There are five tasks of constructive rest and all the others depend on the first, the cultivating of a whole and integrated body awareness. These tasks distinguish constructive rest from plain old rest. For you musicians, constructive rest is even more felicitous than it is for other folks, because the condition one cultivates in constructive rest is the very best condition for practice, rehearsal, and performance.

Most people can build a whole and integrated body awareness best by beginning with the tactile sense, the sense of touch. We have skin all over our bodies loaded with tactile receptors and we have these same receptors interior to our bodies in certain locations, for instance, the nasal passages and the oral cavity. The receptors in the skin give us vital information about temperature, movement of air, pressure, texture, and contact.

People differ greatly in their awareness of tactile sensation. Some people tell me they never lose consciousness of their clothing. They feel it all the time and many say they actively enjoy the sensation of the texture and moving of their clothing throughout the day. Others tell me they are never aware of their clothing, even when they put it on. They know they are dressing, of course, but they are not actively feeling or enjoying the contact with their clothing. Their attention may be absorbed by something else while they dress, the news on the radio, a conversation, planning the day.

Whatever your habit, in constructive rest you want to bring all your tactile sensation directly into awareness and let it live there. Notice the temperature and movement of the air, your clothing, your contact with the floor, parts of your body touching each other, your glasses, the hair on your neck, your watch and jewelry, any sensations of itching or dryness or damp.

Your tactile sense is Janus-faced (Janus was "an ancient Italian deity, regarded by the Romans as presiding over doors and gates and over beginnings and endings, commonly represented with two faces in opposite directions"[25]). It tells you about yourself and it tells you about the world. It tells you about yourself where you leave off and the world begins. It defines your edges, your boundary. It is the location of contact with the floor in constructive rest. It is the boundary of contact with your instrument in practicing. If you can learn good contact with the floor in constructive rest, it will spill over into good contact with your instrument in playing.

Most people who have relinquished their tactile awareness find coming back to it very comforting and reassuring. "It's like coming home," I've been told. Once in a while someone finds it frightening. The boundary seems vulnerable, and, of course, to some degree it *is* vulnerable.

Now, do not give up your tactile sensation, but go interior to it and find your kinesthetic sensation, which is coming from sense receptors of an entirely different kind in entirely different locations. The kinesthetic receptors are in muscle and connective tissue, concentrated at the joints. These receptors flood your brain with information about your position, that is, the relationship of bone to bone. Right now, most of you are in semi-supine position and you know it, thanks to your kinesthetic receptors. Those receptors will be giving that information to your brain whether you are aware of it or not. Now I'm asking you to become aware of your position and of your moving, for instance, the movement of your breathing and of all the micro movement, and to become aware of your size. Fortunately, we have sense receptors to tell us about our size. So, let yourself be fully aware of your position, your movement, and your size. You will also be getting information about whether you are tense, whether you are symmetrical or twisted. Kinesthetic experience ranges, as does tactile, from miserable through delicious. If you're uncomfortably tense, just let yourself be aware of it. Awareness is the means to change. In fact, the only means to change.

It's important to keep the tactile sensation full as you wake up your kinesthesia. You want to really know what's going on in your body, so you need both senses, whole and integrated.

Next, look to be sure that all your emotion is in awareness in all its complexity and intensity. Sometimes we seem to feel only one emotion, but most often we are experiencing a rich braid of emotion. One strand may be bigger or brighter, but there will be other strands. Let yourself be aware of all of them.

Bringing emotion fully into awareness is very important for artists, for emotion plays such a big and vital role in your work. The matter of emotions is complex for musicians, who must be aware of all their own emotion and all the emotion evoked by the music. This is so demanding that some musicians speak of building "emotional muscle," a very useful metaphor, I think.

Now, add to all your tactile, kinesthetic, and emotional awareness anything that falls under the category *Other*—all the pain, if there is any, all the sensations of pleasure, hunger, thirst, anything. Notice, if you have pain, that you can feel pain and feel all the other sensations as well. This is the key to recovery from painful injury and it is the key to managing chronic pain, should you be required to.

People have told me all sorts of things they feel as part of their body awareness that are not included in mine. If you feel things I have not named, like "energy," just let those things live as well in your awareness. There's no reason our awareness shouldn't be as unique as our personalities. The ones I have named—touch, kinesthesia, emotion, pain, pleasure, hunger and thirst—these are essential for practice and performance.

Why are they essential? First because the tactile and kinesthetic and emotional information is crucial to the process of practicing. You're handicapped without it. Second because it takes mental energy to suppress sensation and a kind of splitting or splitting off that is strenuous. It's far easier to feel it than not to feel it.

When you finish any session of constructive rest, you make no effort to keep its benefits. You don't say, for instance, "This is the first time all day my neck has been free, and I'm not going to tense up again." No, that would just introduce some strain. You just get up and go about your business, knowing that your brain will assimilate the experience of constructive rest just the way it assimilates everything else. No need for strain.

Day 2

Remember that the cultivating of a whole and integrated body awareness is the most important task of constructive rest because it is the task on which all the others depend. What are the other tasks? Coming to the greatest degree of muscular freedom you can find in the moment. That's the one we're going to focus on today. Three, working on the integrity of your breathing. Four, developing an accurate and adequate body map. Five, putting yourself in a right relationship with space.

Today, as always, we begin with awareness. As you did yesterday, just find all your tactile sensation, all your kinesthetic sensation, all your emotion, all your other sensations and let them live together. It is this living together in a single gestalt that is what we call integrated. We want all the discrete bits of information in relationship to each other. It's not that you don't know where each is coming from, but it's not in isolation. No pockets of awareness, but letting the gestalt integrate. Then your attention can shift easily among the items in awareness without your losing the others. Some come into focus as others lie on the periphery of attention, waiting to come into focus as they are needed.

Now, please use your awareness to bring yourself to the greatest degree of muscular freedom you can find in the moment. Let yourself register kinesthetically what's going on with regard to tension. Is there muscular tension present? Is it greater in certain parts of your body? Does it form a pattern? Generally people find that they begin to free out of tension as they cultivate awareness. Loss of awareness is one of the main causes of tension. It seems the body doesn't like to be abandoned by awareness.

We know from the observations of F. M. Alexander that the most common pattern of muscular tension is the one he called downward pull, which begins with tension in the muscles of the neck and spreads inevitably to the rest of the body, compressing the body, reducing its stature. Since we know this pattern is the most common one, we do well to come out of it first in constructive rest. Now, this assumes downward pull is present. If it is not, if your neck is nice and free and not imposing tension on the rest of the body, then just enjoy the freedom and see if there are any other patterns of tension you may release out of.

If you find you have neck tension, just begin to address it. You may use Alexander's order to himself, if you like, "I wish my neck to be free." This is a wish in the beginning that over time rises to the status of an intention, so just patiently play with the wish. "I wish my neck to be free."

You may palpate your neck, learning what you can about what is going on that way. You may massage your neck, working with your fingertips all along the base of your skull. You may play with movement, nodding, rocking back, turning gently from side to side to see if you can free your neck in the midst of moving it. As you palpate, be sure you explore the cervical curve. Flattening that curve is a source of all kinds of misery, so you want to be sure you're not flattening and you want to be sure you cultivate and appreciate and protect the natural curve of the neck.

As you find freedom for your neck, let the rest of your body take advantage of it. You may have impulses to movement at that point. You may want to bring your arms over your head or across your chest. You may want to spiral your torso, or move your legs one way or another. You may want to bring your knees to your chest or stretch them out into fully supine. Whatever the impulse, just follow it. You will find that movement in response to impulse almost always frees you. It's the body telling you what it wants. Just answer with movement.

You may find patterns of tension that are peculiar to you. They may come from mismapping, from trauma, from attempts to be shorter or taller. Individual patterns come from all kinds of sources. It may be important for you to understand and resolve the source, it may not. In any case, you can learn to free out of those patterns. Awareness is the key and intention the means.

A few other pointers about constructive rest. We never try to not fall asleep. Assume if you fall asleep that sleep is the most important thing that could be happening. Many people doze off in constructive rest and then just come back awake and go on with what they were doing. If you fear you'll stay asleep and miss a rehearsal, then just set an alarm or a timer.

Also, just because we are thinking about these important tasks does not mean that we can't think about other things as well. Do not censor any thoughts. You can cultivate body awareness and muscular freedom and figure what's going to be on next year's recital or what you're going to have for dinner or where you're going on vacation or what you think about social and political issues. We have brains that can do many things at once and you'll introduce strain if you try to keep from thinking about something. That would just be silly. If you find you've abandoned the tasks, just come back to them. That doesn't mean you'll have to go away from whatever it was you were thinking about that captured all your attention.

When you finish with constructive rest, just get up and go about your business, know that the minutes you spent in constructive rest will not be wasted. Your brain will assimilate them and make them your own over time.

Day 3

Today we work on breathing. Remember that working on breathing is pointless in the absence of a body awareness that is complete enough to really let you know what you are doing. And, we always want to work on breathing in the context of as much muscular freedom as we can find at the moment, because tension interferes with breathing. You will be limited in your work on your breathing by your tension. Nevertheless, you just get as free as you can and then work with your breathing. Very often, you will continue to free generally as you secure better rib movement and better abdominal wall and pelvic floor movement.

So, build your whole and integrated body awareness, use it to become as free as you can in the moment, and then let attention focus on your breathing. How does breathing feel? Is it limited? It's not uncommon for people to be breathing twenty or more times a minute when they first go into constructive rest. It's not uncommon to be breathing six to eight times per minute at the end. This is because the ribs are free to move through a greater excursion, so you get more oxygen with each breath. Since the brain decides when to breathe you again based on chemoreceptors in the blood that monitor oxygen and carbon dioxide, it will need to breathe you less often if the oxygen levels are not frequently low. Is it better to breathe fewer times per minute? I don't know. I know the larger breaths can feel delicious.

Ask yourself whether your breathing seems coordinated or chaotic. Your breathing should be a long, easy sweep of movement top to bottom in the torso, both on inhalation and on exhalation. People who interfere with the natural coordination may even feel something that feels like a reverse of that natural coordination. They are manipulating the abdominal wall, often without even knowing that they are.

Let your attention turn to your rib movement. Let yourself feel the movement of all twenty-four ribs. Let yourself feel the movement at the cost-vertebral joints and at the cartilage in front. Palpate the whole expanse of cartilage along the sternum top to bottom and then on down along the whole reserve V at the top of the abdominal wall. Follow the cartilage all around until you bump up against your floating ribs. If you have ever, ever mapped that region as bone, let yourself appreciate the texture and the movement of the cartilage.

Enjoy the excursion of your ribs up and out on inhalation and then follow the movement down and in on exhalation. Ask yourself whether you are allowing the full excursion down and in. Many singers and wind and brass players stop short of the full excursion in playing.

You don't want to be among them. If you really learn to finish a breath in constructive rest, your learning will carry over to playing, and you will love being able to finish a phrase and a breath at the same time. When you can do this, you will enjoy easy, reflexive inhalations.

Now explore the movement of your abdominal wall in breathing. Remember that we are talking about the abdominal wall front, sides, and back, not just in front. Are you allowing the full movement of the abdominal wall all around in breathing, or is there tension that is interfering? Should there be any tension in the abdominal wall in breathing? No, none, though there will be a lovely dynamic feeling as the muscles spring back on exhalation as pressure from the viscera is reduced.

Constructive rest is an excellent opportunity to explore pelvic floor movement in breathing. You want to be certain there is no interference from tension so that the pelvic floor can be pushed downward on inhalation, and you similarly want no interference from tension on exhalation, so that the pelvic floor can spring back as the pressure comes off. In singing or wind and brass playing, that springing back feels like wonderful support for the breathing, support in the sense of help or aid.

Day 4

As you begin constructive rest today, just do as you have done the last three days and secure for yourself a whole and integrated body awareness to work with, then use it to find as much muscular freedom as you can find today. Be sure that it is freedom that you are chiefly looking for. It's not that you won't know if you're tense. Of course, you will know, and you should know. Still, it's the freedom you want to know about and focus on. After all, someday the tension will be gone and it will be the freedom you will be experiencing, so you should get to know freedom now to whatever degree it is present. This is like always listening for in-tune-ness. If you're out of tune you'll know it and come back on tune, but it's the sense of in-tune-ness you want to be cultivating.

Now, constructive rest is the perfect situation for working on your body map. If your body map is already perfectly accurate and absolutely adequate to your purposes, of course, you will not waste a single minute working on it. If, however, it is inaccurate in some respects, then here's the chance to correct it forever.

Some people work on their body map systematically, using an anatomy book, for instance, from front to back of the book, or going from the top of the head to the fingertips and toes. This is not usual, however, nor necessarily recommended. You can work situationally, on whatever is most important to you at the moment.

Remember that your mapping errors may be in structure, function, or size. Some people will need to be particularly attentive to one arena. Other people find errors spread across the spectrum and must address them all. You can just start with whatever mapping error is interfering most with your performance or your practice or the mapping error that is for whatever reason calling attention to itself.

Begin by knowing as clearly as you can what your mapping has been, then continue on to knowing as clearly as you can what the consequences have been. How has the map affected the movement? Then carefully compare your map with the truth. How does the map differ from the truth? Remember that the truth may be different in structure, or in function, or in size. Now mentally take on the truth. Let the truth truly register in your brain. Now move, letting the truth of the structure or function or size really determine the movement. Let yourself know how the movement differs as the truth determines the movement rather than your old inaccurate map. How exactly does it differ? Let the difference really register in your brain.

You will need to repeat this process in constructive rest and elsewhere until the truth is utterly assimilated into your map and there is no residue of the old inaccuracy and the movement it dictated.

Day 5

This is the day we work on a right relationship to space. We are talking about a right relationship for constructive rest, but that turns out to be just the same as the right relationship for practice and performance, so you are working on your performance right here in constructive rest as you put yourself into genuine relationship with the space around you.

In order to be in a right relationship to space for constructive rest and for practice, you will need an whole and integrated body awareness. This is because we are looking for an inclusive awareness, inclusive of yourself and the world.

There are three basic states you may be in with regard to waking sensory awareness. One is introspective, where all or most of your attention is on yourself. A second is extrospective, where all or most of your attention is on what's outside you, on the world around you. A third is inclusive awareness, in which you are aware of yourself and the world. That's the state or condition we want to cultivate in constructive rest.

You might begin your access to space by looking all around you and putting yourself in relationship to everything you see. "Ah, yes, this is where I am," you say, "in this space." You can go on to let your hearing help you by hearing every available sound and putting yourself in relationship to it. You may use your tactile sense to tell you about the space, the temperature and movement of the air, for instance, the nature of the floor, the continuity of the floor. What can your emotions tell you about the space? Let your emotions really live in relationship to the space.

Now, you can claim for your moving—in this case, your breathing and micro movement—any amount of space you choose. It doesn't need to be confined to the room. You can claim the known universe for your moving if you like, or a space the size of a cathedral. We can be in a tiny practice room and still claim an auditorium-size space for our moving. In fact, you can claim in constructive rest the very space you want to be practicing in, at least as big as the biggest space you ever expect to perform in. This is very important, because if you claim a smaller space for your practicing, then you go out on that concert stage and it's a terrific shock to your nervous system that all that space is there. You don't want shocks to your nervous system at the time of performance, so you consciously practice moving in a space as big as the one you will perform in, or bigger.

Many people learn as they claim larger spaces for their movement that much of their tension came from the small, bubble-like space they were claiming earlier. The small space was the stimulus to which they responded by tensing muscles.

Now, I want to be very clear here about one thing because there is sometimes confusion on this point. I am not talking about imagining the performance space. That would be both difficult and counterproductive in the extreme. You need your imagination for other purposes. I'm talking about claiming in the moment, right here, the same size space you will want to perform in. It's the skill of being in relationship to the space around you. For one thing, an audience will fill that space, and it's your job to be truly in relationship to the audience you are playing for. If you are not in relationship to your audience as you play, we in the audience feel cheated, and we are cheated. It's your business to play for us, not for some abstraction or some entity to which you are refusing attention.

A good, solid, unequivocal relationship to space is one of the great protections against debilitating performance anxiety. Another good reason for cultivating it.

Remember not to introduce any strain into the end of constructive rest. Do not attempt to keep this nice relationship to space. Just go about your business and come back to this as you begin to practice. In practice it will need to be a conscious choice again until it just becomes what you do.

Endnotes

1. Conable, Barbara. *What Every Musician Needs to Know about the Body,* rev. ed. (Portland: Andover Press, 2000), 5.
2. Ibid.
3. Alexander, F. M. *The Use of the Self* (London: Methuen & Co. Ltd., 1932), 103.
4. Conable, 48.
5. http://launch.groups.yahoo.com/group/andovereducators/message/3327 (accessed December 30, 2008).
6. David, Hans T. and Arthur Mendel, eds., *The Bach Reader* (New York: W. W. Norton & Co., 1966), 291.
7. *Marcel Tabuteau's Lessons,* CD, liner notes. Boston Records BR1017, 2001.
8. Caruso, Enrico, and Tetrazzini. *On the Art of Singing* (New York: Dover Publications, 1975), 54.
9. *Bodies: The Exhibition,* catalog (Atlanta: Premier Exhibitions, 2006), 44.
10. Takase, Hiroki and Yutaka Haruki. "Coordination of Breathing between Ribcage and Abdomen in Emotional Arousal." In *Respiration and Emotion,* Yutaka Haruki, I. Homma, A. Umezawa, Y. Masaoka, eds. (Tokyo: Springer-Verlag, 2001).
11. Frederiksen, Brian, Arnold Jacobs: *Song and Wind,* John Taylor, ed. (Gurnee, IL: WindSong Press Limited, 1997), 121–122.
12. Ibid., 119.
13. Ibid., 111.
14. Ibid., 170.
15. *The Oboist's Companion, Volume 2* (Oxford: Oxford University Press, 1976), 18.
16. Mack, John, "Effective Guidance For the Young Oboist." In *The Journal of The International Double Reed Society No. 2,* Gerald Corey and Daniel Stolper, eds. (Boulder, CO: International Double Reed Society, 1974).
17. Robinson, Joe, "Oboists, Exhale Before Playing." In *The Instrumentalist* (Northfield, IL: The Instrumentalist Publishing Co., May, 1987).
18. Fedele, Andrea Lynn. "The Alexander Technique: A Basis for Oboe Performance and Teaching," DMA thesis. (Urbana, IL: University of Illinois at Urbana-Champaign, 2003), 172.
19. Mayer, Lyle Vernon. *Fundamentals of Voice and Diction* (Columbus, OH: McGraw Hill, 1968), 38.
20. Eisenson, Jon, *Voice and Diction: A Program for Improvement,* 7th ed. (Needham Heights, MA: Allyn and Bacon, 1997), 303-304.
21. Ibid., 386.
22. Hewitt, Stevens, *Method for Oboe: 360 Daily Exercises after F. Kroepsch* (self-published, 1973), 93.
23. Eisenson, 319.
24. Mayer, 46.
25. Barnhart, Clarence Lewis, *The American College Dictionary* (New York: Random House, 1966.)

Bibliography

To further your understanding of Oboemotions.

Alexander, F. M. *The Use of the Self: Its Conscious Direction in Relation to Diagnosis Functioning and the Control of Reaction.* Reissued. London: Orion Books Ltd., 2001.

Blakeslee, Sandra and Matthew Blakeslee. *The Body Has a Mind of its Own: How Body Maps in Your Brain Help You Do (Almost) Everything Better.* New York: Random House, 2007.

Conable, Barbara. *What Every Musician Needs to Know about the Body: The Practical Application of Body Mapping to Making Music.* Rev. ed. Portland, OR: Andover Press, 2000.

_____. *The Structures and Movement of Breathing: A Primer for Choirs and Choruses.* Chicago: GIA Publications, Inc. 2000.

Conable, Barbara, and William Conable. *How to Learn the Alexander Technique: A Manual for Students.* 3rd ed. Columbus, OH: Andover Press, 1995.

Dawson, William J. *Fit as a Fiddle: The Musician's Guide to Playing Healthy.* Lanham, MD: Rowman & Littlefield Education, 2008.

Dimon, Jr., Theodore. *Anatomy of the Moving Body: A Basic Course in Bones, Muscles, and Joints.* Berkeley, CA: North Atlantic Books, 2001.

Fedele, Andrea Lynn. *The Alexander Technique: A Basis for Oboe Performance and Teaching.* DMA thesis. Urbana, IL: University of Illinois at Urbana-Champaign, 2003.

Frederiksen, Brian. *Arnold Jacobs: Song and Wind.* John Taylor, ed. Gurnee, IL: WindSong Press Limited, 1997.

Gilmore, Robin. *What Every Dancer Needs to Know about the Body.* Portland, OR: Andover Press, 2005.

Gorman, David. *The Body Moveable.* Guelph, Ontario: Ampersand Printing Co., 1981.

Hooper, Kay. *Sensory Tune-ups: A Guided Journal of Sensory Experiences for Performers of All Ages.* Selinsgrove, PA: AllSense Press, 2005 (available at www.allsensepress.com).

Kapit, Wynn, and Lawrence M. Elson. *The Anatomy Coloring Book.* 3rd ed. San Francisco: Benjamin Cummings, 2001.

Koch, Rolf Julius. *The Technique of Oboe Playing.* Mainz: Shott Music, 1990.

Malde, Melissa, Mary Jean Allen, and Kurt Alexander Zeller. *What Every Singer Needs to Know about the Body.* San Diego, CA: Plural Publishing, Inc., 2009.

Mark, Thomas. *What Every Pianist Needs to Know about the Body.* Chicago: GIA Publications, Inc., 2004.

Pearson, Lea. *Body Mapping for Flutists: What Every Flute Teacher Needs to Know about the Body*. Chicago: GIA Publications, Inc., 2006.

Vining, David. *What Every Trombonist Needs to Know about the Body*. Kagarice Brass Editions, 2009. (Order at www.kagarice.com.)

More information about Body Mapping (including useful articles, workshops, and a list of certified Andover Educators) is found at www.bodymap.org

About the Author

Oboist Stephen Caplan, a successful performer of solo, chamber, and orchestral music, is also recognized for outstanding teaching. His solo recording of American music for oboe and English horn, *A Tree in Your Ear*, has received international acclaim. *Fanfare* describes it as "sublime" and *Double Reed News* writes, "beautifully played...it is hard to imagine anyone not enjoying this CD."

Raised in central Louisiana, Caplan began playing the oboe when he was twelve and was soon winning competitions and studying with some of America's leading teachers. While in high school he was a concerto winner with the New Orleans Philharmonic and a national finalist in the Music Teachers National Association's Young Artist Competition. Caplan received an undergraduate degree in music performance from Northwestern University, and MM and DMA degrees from The University of Michigan. He studied primarily with Ray Still, Arno Mariotti, and Harry Sargous, and was also influenced by musical studies with the tuba player, Arnold Jacobs and the flutist, Marcel Moyse.

Stephen Caplan is now Professor of Oboe at the University of Nevada, Las Vegas and serves as Principal Oboist of the Las Vegas Philharmonic. His eclectic performance background includes professional affiliations with a Baroque period instrument ensemble and a Sousa-style concert band, as well as soundtracks for television and film. His performances have been heard on National Public Radio's *All Things Considered* and *Performance Today*, and at venues such as the Kennedy Center and Carnegie Hall. He is an Artist for *Rigoutat, Paris*, one of the world's leading oboe manufacturers, and has appeared as a concerto soloist with orchestras throughout the United States and Europe. With the chamber ensemble Sierra Winds, Caplan performs on five critically acclaimed recordings and has been the recipient of numerous grants and awards, including the Nevada Governor's Award for Excellence in the Arts. He has also played in orchestras on the Las Vegas Strip, accompanying a diverse group of popular and classical superstars from Tony Bennett and Ray Charles to Luciano Pavarotti.

In 2004 Caplan became a certified Andover Educator after extensive private study with Barbara Conable. He now teaches undergraduate and graduate level courses on Body Mapping and Music Wellness at UNLV. His "Oboemotions" master class has been featured at conferences of the International Double Reed Society, and he has authored several articles for *The Double Reed* and other journals. He has been a clinician for Nora Post's Oboe Blowout, Northwest Oboe Seminar, and California Double Reed Day. In addition, Caplan has given master classes at many of the leading music schools in the United States.